INDEPENDENCE
LADY

INDEPENDENCE
LADY

•

MONICA COGLAS

AVALON BOOKS
THOMAS BOUREGY AND COMPANY, INC.
401 LAFAYETTE STREET
NEW YORK, NEW YORK 10003

PRINTED IN THE UNITED STATES OF AMERICA
ON ACID-FREE PAPER
BY HADDON CRAFTSMEN, SCRANTON, PENNSYLVANIA

I would like to dedicate this book, first of all, to the Lord Jesus
Christ,
who gave me new life and a precious gift of writing.
Also, to Tina Carter who has been my kindred-heart friend
for many years.
I thank my parents, Marvin and Loraine Rieken,
for being so encouraging when I told them I wanted to become a
writer.
And I also appreciate and thank my husband, Len,
whose support and patience helped me attain this goal. Thank you
all, for your love.

Chapter One

"This is insane," Amanda grumbled. She swung hopelessly at the lemon-yellow ball and missed again. *You must . . . be mental,* she said to herself, huffing for oxygen. She swiped her brow and pushed the long black bangs away from her eyes. Her ambition to learn tennis was becoming more taxing than expected. *At least it's my choice,* she thought, tired of living by her father's wishes since her mother's death.

Amanda had eagerly joined Faircastle Resort after moving to Virginia with her father. She'd willingly left England behind at twenty-three. Her past was over; it was time to make a change. Of course, tennis lessons couldn't equal pursuing her dream. That was next. But initiating the lessons was a step in the right direction, she was certain.

Winded, she prepared for the next shot. She focused

1

on the machine. *Two left. I must hit one.* The next ball popped out, zooming straight at her. She swung, but sent it down to bounce painfully off her ankle.

"Ooh!" She rubbed her foot. *You've learned this before,* she reproved herself for not concentrating. Once more she waited for the onslaught. The ball popped out and whizzed toward her. She swung with determination, and met the ball with a resounding *whop.* It sailed beautifully over the net and bounced just inside the corner of the court. Amanda stared in shock. Then the joy of victory bubbled up inside and made her smile.

"Good shot," a masculine voice carried from one court over.

She turned to see an athletic man, tall and tanned. He trotted onto her court, grinning. His teeth glistened like sugar on his honey-brown face.

Amanda took a deep breath. "Thanks, but you didn't see my blunders before that," she said. He laughed, a hearty chuckle, full of empathy and warmth.

"Amanda Chambers?" he asked, examining her like a long-lost friend.

"Yes." She nodded, shielding her eyes from the sun.

"Brandon Cordell." He extended a muscular arm and pressed his warm hand gently against hers in a shake. "I'm your instructor."

She gazed, surprised. When he said his name she'd felt a faint sliver of recognition, like déjà vu. But they couldn't have met before; she'd recently moved to the United States. Or could they?

"You're going to have your hands full. I'm not very good," she said.

He shrugged off her warning. "That's why you're here, right?"

"Yes." No. He wasn't even close. But it didn't matter. Her private struggle to become independent from her oppressive father was her concern.

"Your registration says you've recently moved from London. Welcome."

"Thank you. Charlottesville, Virginia, is beautiful."

He nodded. "You know"—he leaned nearer—"after living here a while you won't want to move back to England."

Distracted by the nearness of his clean-shaven face, her response lodged in her throat tighter than a champagne cork. She only blinked.

"Looks like you've warmed up. Let's see what your swings are *really* like." He winked, confessing his teasing air. Then, with another broad smile, he turned and jogged across court. Amanda watched in a stupor. Her stomach tumbled. It wasn't the lessons anymore that parked her nerves on edge. It was this man. She feared embarrassing herself. He was so . . . distracting.

As he selected a handful of balls she took a deep breath, trying to focus. He lobbed several balls, but her swings sent most of them straight into the net. Other times she missed them entirely.

Amanda frowned; her concentration was slipping. She bit her lip and fixed her gaze on the ball. He played a slow serve, but it was a far stretch to her right. Jolting into motion she swung in the nick of time, but it was too strong and she watched the ball soar over the chain-link fence.

"Bother!" She winced at her blatant error. As she

turned toward the back line she felt her skirt shifting. "What—? No!" she whispered, discovering that the emphatic swing had dislodged her zipper. She glanced in the instructor's direction and balanced her racket between her knees, trying to refasten the zipper. But her yanking only made it catch.

Please! she begged silently. She knew the scene looked awkward and saw her instructor reapproaching her court. Adrenaline poured like ice water through her veins. *Quick. Do it up!* Her hands busily at work behind her, she watched as he examined her situation. Heat crawled into her cheeks.

"Is something wrong? Did you hurt your back?" His face showed concern.

"No ... I'm not hurt." Amanda blushed, trying to maintain her balance and keep her back hidden from him. "I'm ... well, I'm afraid that I'm ... undone."

"Undone?" he said, his head cocked to the side, then his smile spread in a show of insight. "I see." He nodded. "Need help?" His grin softened with the offer.

"No!" She moved backward. "It just needs ... there ... no—"

"Sure? I promise to be a gentleman."

She studied his face, knowing she didn't have much choice, unless she ran all the way back to the dressing rooms.

"You may as well let me try." His sincerity flowed. "Besides, you'll never learn any technique like that."

His words communicated more than tact. They were truth.

"All right," Amanda whispered, "but please be discreet, will you?" She retrieved her racket and turned her back to him, looking anxiously to see if anyone was watching before she released the zipper.

"If you don't let go, I can't help," he said softly.

"Sorry." Hesitantly, she relaxed her grip, thankful that the zipper had caught high enough that the only thing showing was her embarrassment.

"Your waist is so tiny."

She flushed. How did she manage to fall into these predicaments? "Hurry, please."

"You do eat, don't you?"

"I'm a ballerina in the Regis Ballet Company," she answered. "Starving us is only one of their rules." For a fleeting moment, she'd let herself cross into territory that was taboo for the weekend—ballet. Endless rehearsals and expectations. The demanding profession had finally exhausted her patience. She had to get out. But could she?

The instructor tugged a few times. She could feel the light brushing of his fingers working next to her waist. It tickled and she bit her lip to keep from laughing.

"You know," he talked just behind her ear, "that accent of yours is elegant. It suits you." With another tug the zipper moved freely. "There."

"Oh, thank—" She turned and glanced up at him. Her appreciation faded into marvel as she looked into his intense blue eyes—so clear and gorgeous they looked bottomless, like tropical ocean waters.

"My pleasure, Amanda," he finally said, and his smile returned. "Worthy of love."

"Pardon?"

"Your name—Amanda. It means worthy of love."

She looked away, feeling a tingle race down to her

toes. How could she let a strange man help with her zipper in broad daylight? The warmth in her face finally receded and she faced him confidently. "Shall we continue?"

"Absolutely."

Amanda tried to hide her wavering, but keeping her concentration wasn't going to be easy with those eyes of his. But it was necessary.

She watched him walk back. A row of sable curls bounced along his neck. With each stride, leg muscles knotted from training. Her breath caught as she admired his good looks. Finally she forced herself to inhale.

She willed herself to concentrate on tennis. It was possible—as long as Brandon Cordell was across court. But to her surprise he only retrieved the cart of balls and started to cross back. She blinked. Her last hope for concentration disintegrated.

"Now that I have an idea of your skill level," he said, "it's time to show you some basic swings." Brandon stood beside her and lifted her arm to demonstrate a return swing. The fresh scent of his aftershave frazzled her thoughts. She wondered if she should give up on the idea of learning tennis.

Like a master, he taught her professional grips, turns, and technique. He continually positioned her body into stances and angles. Every time he touched her Amanda felt a tingle, and every ball she hit seemed to go straight through her racquet strings. All she could focus on was him, and the more she did so, the more clumsily she reacted.

Amanda finally decided she'd had enough. "I think

you've given me plenty to think about until next week,'' she said, trying to look cheerful.

"You still have a half hour."

"It's better if I stop. Besides, my hand is getting sore." She glanced at the reddened palm and Brandon reached for her hand to inspect it. She tensed at his grasp, but the strength and warmth of his touch soon caused her to relax. He gently rubbed a finger along the worn spot. His tenderness surprised her and she watched his brows furrow from his concern.

"Yep. You'll have a blister tomorrow. I've got some gauze and tape in my office. I'll wrap it for you."

"No." She tugged her hand back, not meaning to jerk it so quickly. "I mean, thank you, but I'll be fine." What she really wanted was to leave the club as gracefully as possible and forget her blunders in front of this attractive man. It was enough that she melted when he touched her. To be doctored by him was more than she could handle. "Really, I've tended plenty of wounds, thanks to ballet."

He stared. "Doesn't sound like a fun career. I take it you're not happy with your choice."

It hadn't been *her* choice. Amanda really didn't want to travel down this path of topics but she'd mentioned it. "Tennis would have been better. If I could learn how to swing," she said dryly.

"You did well. But you've played before."

She gaped at him, wondering how he guessed. "Yes, several years ago, in England. During one of my father's publishing seminars. How did you know?"

He cleared his throat. "You bear the rusty marks of former training."

She squinted, then reflected on years past. "Some kind man noticed my desperation. I missed every ball. He took pity on me and spent most of the day showing me tips."

"Lucky guy. I only got half an hour."

Amanda enjoyed his playful smile, but something in his voice made her backbone shiver. There was something familiar about him.

"So, next Saturday, Amanda?"

If his grin had been any more alluring she'd have fainted. She gave a quick nod and turned for the locker room.

While freshening up, her thoughts floated back to Brandon. She could swear she'd met him before. But where? It couldn't be. He'd have mentioned it.

Amanda passed the lobby, seeing a sandwich-board sign announcing an Independence Day dance: *Celebrate the Freedom,* it declared in bold letters. She groaned in response to its claim. Freedom. She yearned for it. When would her father realize she was a grown woman and stop trying to control her life? She pushed the resentment away and kept walking.

She realized then that she had another thirty minutes before Barclay would show so she went in the gazebo-shaped lounge to wait. The small lounge was sectioned off to one side of the clubhouse. Lush vines climbed the wood lattice making its atmosphere semiprivate. In the empty room she selected a table by the plant-covered railing and placed her tote bag at her feet.

The waiter appeared. "Afternoon, miss. What would you like?" He set down a blue paper cylinder that spelled the resort name in bright gold.

Amanda ordered a raspberry seltzer. The lounge reminded her of cohosting her father's numerous functions for the publishing house. They were well stocked for Jonathan Chambers' staff, editors, and fellow publishers. She enjoyed standing by her father's side while listening to the professionals discussing their role in the business. She'd learned plenty about business hazards by giving ear to others' hard experience.

Yet, since their cross-continental move there hadn't been any functions. Not yet, anyway. Jonathan had recently scheduled one to introduce himself as the new owner of the small Huntington House. Last week, he and Amanda had jointly signed and mailed the invitations, according to their usual custom.

The waiter brought her seltzer, giving her a friendly smile. He laid some paperwork on the edge of the table. ''So, you're a new member?''

She nodded stiffly. ''Does it show?'' she asked, watching him chuckle.

''Not in a bad way. But I certainly would have remembered a lady as lovely as you.'' He smiled again and went back to his post behind the bar.

Hearing his appreciation, she figured everyone on the resort staff was trained to make the members feel special. She took a long sip of the iced beverage and mused over some of the comments Brandon had made. A funny feeling twisted in her belly. She was certain he was showing more than hospitality—more like *interest.* Yet what unsettled her more was that she still couldn't place whether she'd met him before.

Thoughts drifting, she peeked over the entwined plants

to watch as people filtered through the lobby. Her wandering gaze halted at a familiar face. Brandon. It was hard to miss him; his appearance stood out in the crowd. His dynamic smile and white clothes enhanced his sun-darkened, muscular physique. With the distance between them, she braved staring, thinking she'd be undetected. She watched him talk with various members, shake hands with the men and greet women with a casual, surveying glance. She sensed intelligence in him, but there was more than mere smarts—strength and sensitivity flowed with every move he made. They were genuine actions, the kind you knew stemmed from bona fide inner qualities. She wondered if his kisses were as strong and sensitive, and suddenly he glanced her way, catching her staring.

Amanda yanked her chin down toward her drink, almost hunching herself over the tall glass. *You fool. Now he'll think I'm silly over him.* She spun the miniature blue umbrella between her thumb and forefinger and waited.

''Would you like another one?''

Brandon's voice sent a shiver down her spine, and she sat up to meet his smiling face. ''No thank you. I don't think that would be a good idea. I mean, its nice of you to offer, but this was plenty.''

''Mind if I join you, then?''

He rested a golden-brown hand on the chair beside her. Between his close stance and the interest in his eyes, Amanda struggled to keep from feeling like a teenager. He waited for her approval and she didn't want to be rude.

''Please.'' She gestured to the chair and resumed fidgeting with the tiny umbrella. Keeping up her guard on the court had been easier; she had a purpose for being there. But now he'd caught her staring and it'd be difficult to pretend it hadn't happened. "Actually, I'm waiting for someone."

The waiter appeared and Brandon ordered a soda. Once the waiter left, Brandon leaned closer to her.

"Your chauffeur?" he said, tilting one eyebrow and watching her.

She blinked in surprise. "How did you know?" she asked, a little uncomfortable with his knowledge of her pampered status.

"It's Jonathan Chambers' way."

Amanda stared back, questions filling her mind. "You know my father?"

He paused and reclined in the wood chair, then grinned. "Just a hunch. Treating you special would be my way too, Amanda."

She stirred the ice chips around in her glass. Now she wasn't sure which made her more nervous: his interest in her, or the hint that he knew her father and was reluctant to explain. She studied his face and sensed the strange, familiar feelings again. Whenever she looked into his eyes a vague memory tugged her recollection. Each time it surfaced it got a little clearer, like she was closer to remembering. Then she pushed the thought away. How could she know him, with their different homelands?

"How long have you been an instructor here?" she asked.

"Too long. Full time, until last year. Now it's just on

Saturdays. I have other plans on the horizon that I've waited a long time for.''

''I empathize with you. I have my own dreams of owning purebred horses and running a riding-stable business.''

''Really?'' He tilted his head, attentive to her.

''Absolutely. Ever since I went riding for the first time.'' Amanda sighed. Her peace started fading and regret spread through her like an unwanted disease. ''I would have traded my whole life for a fine horse then.''

''And now?''

''Now . . . ?'' Her gaze drifted down to her ice chips and a scene of disaster flashed in her mind. The horrid memory was still so fresh, though its wounds were years old. Realizing her delay she finally answered, ''Yes, even now. It's just—well, it's not that easy.'' She saw Brandon studying her face with searching eyes, and she hoped he wouldn't ask her to explain.

''Hmm,'' he said, offering her a tender smile.

''So, no tennis elbow on your agenda?'' she said, trying to change the subject.

Brandon gave a hearty laugh and it echoed in the vacant lounge. ''No way. In fact, this is my last season as instructor. I own a business a little south of here.''

The waiter delivered Brandon's drink and left.

''Are you merely resigning, or relocating?'' Amanda asked.

''Both. As soon as I sell my resort condo I'll resign.''

''Why would you sacrifice living in this beautiful place?''

Brandon folded his hands and leaned nearer, inches from her face. ''Because I've found the perfect place,'' he answered in a low, partial whisper, as though it was top secret. Then he grinned and tipped his glass for a long swallow.

He licked the moisture off his lips. Amanda felt her lungs constrict and a sudden warmth flash through her. *How does he do this to me?* She moved back a little from his alluring gaze, trying to redirect her thinking.

"And you own this perfect place, I gather?"

"Yep. I call it my paradise."

"Really? That must be something to see."

"I'd like that."

"What?"

"For you to see it."

Amanda shook her head. "No—I didn't mean to invite myself."

"I'm serious."

Her gaze locked with his. She couldn't imagine spending time alone with him. He was so attractive it was dangerous. "No. I don't think—"

"Why not?" His smile was broad, his eyes dark and perceptive. "You're not referring to the club's rule of propriety? They frown on those contacts, but I wouldn't lose my job." He waited in silence.

Amanda felt her remaining breath seep out. He was too good at cat-and-mouse. He'd chased her into a corner, and getting out of it would be difficult. Struggling for nonchalance, she thought of a way to pop his confidence. "And how many others have seen your paradise, Brandon?"

"As in female? None."

"None?" She laughed. It wasn't the answer she'd expected. "I don't believe you."

"You don't have to, but it's true."

"Then . . . why me?"

He paused, leaning nearer to her again. "Because I created it with someone like you in mind, Amanda. Pure beauty. I know you'll like it."

She smiled cynically, figuring he'd have dreamt up a more convincing line. "You're very certain of that?"

"Positive."

His alluring gaze was too strong for her and she straightened in her wooden chair. He was too sure of everything. She felt her resistance shaving down to a thin layer. She lifted her glass, taking in ice chips to chew on as she watched him, his assurance never wavering.

"You'd have no interest in me. I'm just another rich club member, who must be pampered and chauffeured to every destination."

Brandon laughed again, this time looking surprised. "Not even close. You are a beautiful, sensitive woman, and it's my opinion you just need a little influence to break out of your father's shadow."

"Shadow?" She peered at him. "You *do* know my father, don't you?"

He paused. "Maybe more than you think. But that's not important."

Amanda scrunched her brow, searching his face for clues. Was he being honest? She wanted to question him further but she saw Barclay entering the lobby and it interrupted her train of thought.

"We'll have to finish this another time. My ride is here." She fished out her wallet to pay for her drink, but Brandon placed his hand over hers.

"My treat. For letting me infringe upon your time."
He smiled, signed the paperwork, and then stood to help
with her chair.

Amanda stood beside him, momentarily trapped in the
tiny space between Brandon, the lattice wall, and the
table. Her modest height brought her just below his chin
and she could smell a hint of that aftershave. The nearness toyed with her thinking. She mentally tasted the
cool sweetness of his lips and the thought launched her
heartbeat into double time.

"You'll think about my offer?" he said in a lowered
voice.

Amanda looked into captivating blue eyes. "I—I'll
think about it."

She didn't recall forming the words, but she knew they
didn't just come out on their own. His persuasion completely squashed her nonchalance and replaced it with
desire, flaming her cheeks. She excused herself, hoping
he hadn't noticed her attraction to him.

Brandon, she mused during the ride home, watching
the lush Virginia hillside country pass by in a green motion picture. *There's something about him that's too confident and too mysterious . . . like he knows something
about me.* Just remembering his gaze tied her stomach
in knots. She was amazed at how he could be so in tune
with her thoughts, or had it only seemed that way?

Whatever the case, Amanda held genuine interest in
seeing his paradise. She'd often dreamed of having a
beautiful place to call her own, away from her father's
watchful eye. But uncertainty sprinkled through her as
she imagined being alone with Brandon in a place

charming enough to be called paradise. For now, she decided, it'd be wise to keep her mind off Brandon—and his paradise—and focus on important things. Like changing her relationship with her sheltering father.

Chapter Two

Amanda jolted as bottle rockets whistled and burst from the house across the way. Though there were two blocks between houses, the noises carried easily over the grasslands. She put her hand to her chest and sighed to relax. "Better get used to it," she muttered. The fireworks stands had opened and it was another three weeks before the Fourth of July.

Distracted from her book she placed it on the parlor coffee table. Reading was hopeless, anyway. Her attention was elsewhere—Brandon. It was impossible to forget his face and their conversation about paradise. His smile kept flashing in her mind, and it triggered the mysterious déjà vu she'd felt around him earlier.

Now almost sundown, it was time for her usual walk. She tried to never miss watching the sunset. It was her

time, when she reflected on her mother's final words . . .
that Amanda must pursue her dreams.

She walked a steady pace up the hill of the back acre
and hoped this peculiar inkling over Brandon wouldn't
trip her up during rehearsal. Her new ballet company
demanded meticulous concentration. Even the slightest
distraction provoked her instructor's wrath. One thing
was in her favor, though. With the nearing Independence
Day came a holiday—one she'd never celebrated before—and she would take any holiday she could from
ballet.

She sat in the grass, watching the cloudy sky transpose
from peach to fuchsia, then violet. Its striking colors
deepened the face of the grassland to a dark emerald.
Huge clouds sailed the horizon. Guided by the increasing
wind they tumbled together and folded into diverse
shapes. She reflected on their dramatic display, rolling
by, swelling with the threat of rain but not releasing any.
They depicted a strange parallel to her own life: recurring frustrations with her father, dreams enlarging in her
heart . . . yet no freedom to fulfill what she felt destined
to do.

She watched the last strip of navy-purple fade into
blackness. The wind had picked up considerably and it
tossed her hair against her face. The air had that certain
ominous smell of a rainstorm. A harrowing memory resurfaced of another storm, and Amanda's pulse quickened. It spoiled her serenity and she rose quickly,
heading back to the house.

Freezing wind howled in Amanda's ears and trees
whisked past in a shadowy green blur. Her nose ran from

the icy air. Pelting rain stung her eyes, making it impossible to watch where she was directing the horse. The gelding jerked and pulled to avoid approaching trees. His nostrils puffed shafts of white steam. She wouldn't dare make him go any faster lest she run them both into a tree. The rain battered her face in unrelenting sheets. Amanda knew she'd have to slow down or—

Whack! A menacing blow struck her forehead. It throbbed. Her ride halted in a painful, spinning halt. She knew she'd been knocked to the ground, and she tried to sit up. But she couldn't move. Then blackness swept over her, compelling her to scream....

"I'm-m c-cold," Amanda whispered through chattering teeth, trembling from the shivers racking her wet, chilled body. Her limbs were numb and her incessant chattering made her head pound with a vengeance.

She thought she heard a voice—no, two voices. Then a bright light pierced her eyes with its radiance, intensifying the throb.

"Hey, she's comin' around. Look! She blinked."

"Ugh! Th-that . . . awful . . . light." She conquered her chattering enough to speak, but found another stabbing pang constricted her breathing.

"You're right. Let's get her out of here."

"Please . . . stop shining . . . light . . . my eyes." Amanda lifted a wounded hand to shield her vision from the intrusion.

"It's all right, love. We 'ad to check your pupils. Now we're going to put you on the stretcher. I want you to cross your arms like this."

In the darkness she felt the paramedic fold her arms.

Something heavy and warm fell across her and straps secured her to the board. Then the two men lifted her gently. Squeaky wheels wobbled along the metal floor of the ambulance and Amanda realized she was going to the hospital.

"Wait! The horse!" she yelled, trying to sit up despite the belts.

"Hold on, love. Your horse is fine. 'E already made it back to the stables. That's when we started searchin' for you."

Amanda finally closed her eyes, thankful. She heard the dull clamp of the ambulance door and the vehicle soon started off on a bumpy backwoods ride.

"I tried . . . to scream. But everything . . . went black."

"You're safe now. But we need to look at that bump. You've been out there a pitiful long while."

"How . . . long?" She moaned, feeling warmer now with the blanket.

" 'Least four hours."

She was dumbfounded. All that time had seemed like seconds.

"Now, let me take a closer look at your forehead. Hmm, that bump's a whopper. Be a while before the swellin' goes down."

The ache in Amanda's heart was twice as menacing as the one in her head. "My father must be petrified. He'll never let me ride again."

"Hey, hey! There's no need to work yourself up. I'm sure he's goin' to be grateful you're still alive. Accidents happen." He paused. "Now, your head'll hurt a lot less if you'd just try to relax."

She felt the relief of smoother traveling on paved road, and her chaperoned journey was accented by the wail of sirens. In spite of the paramedic's comforting words, tears seeped from her eyes and rolled down her cheeks. She knew it would be a long time before she made it back to the stables . . . a *very* long time.

Amanda woke with a start, sweating and trembling from the nightmare.

"*No!*" She released a shaky whimper and pushed off the dampened sheets. She gaped at her shrouded bedroom. A flash lit the interior, and thunder boomed and crackled. She recalled leaving the double-decker window open for some night air, as she wasn't yet accustomed to Virginia's summer heat.

She squinted at her bedside clock. Eight-fifteen. It seemed much earlier in the foreboding shadows cast by the storm. Amanda got up to close the window, then peered through the diamond-patterned panes at the now-muted storm.

The dream. It had plagued her so often after the accident in London. Always the same scene. Always waking her in a drenched sweat. But years had passed since its last recurrence. She'd assumed it was over. Until now.

"Will it never end?" she whispered.

But she knew why it had returned. Brandon opened the lid to Pandora's box yesterday. And Amanda knew it was time to talk to her father. She had to ride again, if only to terminate the nightmares once and for all. Six years had passed since the accident, when her father forbade her to ride anymore. Amanda's heart had broken. But when he then decided that she should study ballet, she knew her hopes of owning a stable business were slowly being eliminated. She wanted to protest. Except one didn't challenge Jonathan Chambers. Once made, his decisions were permanent.

Until now. She was twenty-three. He had to let go. He should have done so years ago. But he was too stubborn, and she didn't want to see him hurt by a nasty rebellion. So, ballet it was.

Amanda turned. Her foot squished in cold, wet carpet.

"Oh! What a mess." She checked the windowsill and saw the water stream trickling from the corner of the ledge onto the thick carpet. She switched on the light and grabbed a towel to soak up the water, but it wasn't enough. She donned her white velour robe and opened the bedroom door.

"Sara?" she called down the vast, curved flight of stairs. "Could you please come here?"

"Yes, Amanda?" the woman trilled from the downstairs hall. She came bustling up the stairs and stood attentively in her pearl-gray dress and white apron, the housekeeper attire Jonathan Chambers had insisted on for two decades. Wide-eyed and panting, she gaped, "What is it, dear?"

"There's a puddle on the rug from the storm. I tried toweling it but it's too substantial. Please help me and grab a sponge and pail, before a stain sets."

"Certainly. Right away."

Amanda watched the aging woman bustle down the stairs. Sara's dark-brown hair, now streaked with silver, bounced in its bun with each quick step. Though plump and short, she was strong and very kind. Amanda held the deepest respect, appreciation, and fondness for their housekeeper/cook. Through the years, and especially after Amanda's mother died, Sara had become more than a loyal employee, she'd also become a close friend.

Amanda retrieved another towel from the bathroom. Sara soon walked in carting supplies. On their knees they sponged together.

"No need for you to fuss, Amanda. This won't take a minute."

"Don't be silly. You know I like to help you. I think we caught it soon enough." Amanda doubled up the towel as Sara sopped beside her. Sara wrung the swollen sponge with an ardent squeeze and thunder rumbled another threat. Amanda's concentration drifted as she stared out the window.

"Thinking about something, dear?"

She nodded. "I had another dream . . . about the accident."

Shock replaced Sara's look of curiosity, and she ceased her sponging. "But you haven't had that dream for years!" Her gaping softened and she stared at Amanda with sympathy. "Is the ballet upsetting you again?"

"No more than usual."

"Perhaps it was caused by the rain?" Sara asked.

"Perhaps." But Amanda knew why the issue had resurfaced. Brandon's talk of freeing herself from her father had greatly stirred old memories. She'd even confessed her feelings about riding to him.

Sara's eyebrows drew together and she scrubbed at the rug. "I think you're just under too much stress with these long rehearsals, and that audition coming up in September."

True. Rehearsals and auditions were the top two on Amanda's "most dreaded" list. It didn't matter any longer that ballet made her father happy. She'd reached the end of her tolerance. She'd truly give up everything to own a fine horse, just as she'd said to Brandon. Over the years, none of her dreams had changed. And verbalizing her ambitions only made the flame burn stronger.

"With all respect, Amanda, I think this has been bothering you for too long. Perhaps it's time to talk to Mr. Chambers."

Amanda gave a mocking laugh. Talk to him? Nobody talked *to* her father. "I thought of that immediately, Sara. You know I've tried."

"Yes, but that was so many years ago. You're a grown woman now. He's sure to be more understanding this time." She plopped the sponge into the pail and it bobbed in the water.

"For years he's never even mentioned it. The accident caused him so many fears, I don't think he'll ever risk it again. Not if he can help it."

"That's why it'll have to start with you, Amanda."

Amanda knew only too well her father would never suggest that she try riding again. The law had been laid down when she'd returned from the hospital, and he'd never wavered in his thinking. Now, after an era of silence, she wasn't sure how to take that first step in talking to him.

She frowned and crossed over to her dressing table. She sat in front of the mirror and tilted her head to bring the thick, sable hair to one side. She brushed rhythmically to the pattering of rain against her window. Then she sectioned off three handfuls to start a French braid.

"Would you like me to weave your braid?" Sara had finished sponging up the rug, and stood pail in one hand, sponge in the other.

Amanda smiled. "Thank you. You know how I end up with knots."

Sara brushed through Amanda's long hair and began weaving and twisting with experienced fingers. When she quickly finished she patted Amanda's shoulders. "I'll start you a bath. Then I'm back to slicing melons."

Inspecting the braid, Amanda saw the perfect twists. "You're too good to me, Sara. No man will have me so spoiled."

Sara paused at the doorway, looking frank. "No man should treat you any less, if he's any man at all." She then ambled down the hallway.

Amanda mulled over the advice until the blast of running water broke into her thoughts. She headed for the bathroom. As the tub filled, she sat on the edge and pinned up her braid. This was her thinking spot. The large private bath upstairs was her favorite place to relax and dream about her future. She slipped out of her robe and sank below the steaming water. Then she closed her eyes, hearing only the muted snapping of foamy bubbles.

Finally. She sighed. The water's heat soothed the tightness in her overworked legs, but there were still nine weeks before summer preparation ended, and she knew the rehearsals ahead would be the toughest yet.

Not wanting to dwell on her dreadful summer schedule, she dreamed instead of what life would be like free of ballet.

After the bath, Amanda wrapped herself in a soft,

emerald-green bath towel. She wandered to her bedroom. As she passed the upstairs telephone it rang, startling her.

"Hello?" she answered.

"Amanda?"

Her pulse quickened when she recognized the male voice.

"Yes. Hello, Brandon."

"Hi. I wanted to tell you that you left your tote bag under the table yesterday. I thought you might be wondering where it was. Sorry I didn't contact you last night."

"Oh!" Amanda laughed. "I completely forgot. I'm thankful that you called. My watch is in the bag."

"I'd be happy to stick around the club for a while. But I'm expecting a call. As soon as it comes through, I'll be leaving for my cabin. Or I can keep your bag locked in my office until your next lesson."

That wouldn't do, she thought. She needed her watch at rehearsals. "No, I'll come pick it up. This morning is best for me. It's a little bit of a drive, though. Is half an hour too long to keep you?"

"Not at all. I'll meet you in the lobby at ten o'clock."

"All right. Good-bye." She replaced the receiver and hurried to get dressed. Since it was Sunday, Barclay was off and she'd have the pleasure of driving herself to the club. She loathed being carted everywhere. She'd often complained that they may as well have used a baby buggy. Besides, there wasn't sense in having passed the Virginia licensing exam if she never had a chance to drive.

Amanda arrived at the clubhouse three minutes before ten, just as the rain came to a halt. Sunlight cut through the dark clouds and made everything sparkle. She glanced around the busy lobby, checking each face for those handsome features, and she realized her anxiousness to see Brandon again.

"Looking for the perfect match?"

She jumped at the provocative voice instantly behind her. Spinning around she saw Brandon standing in khaki shorts and an emerald cotton jersey. Why did he always look so desirable?

"Sorry." He lowered his voice to above a whisper. "I hadn't planned on giving you mouth-to-mouth resuscitation."

Embarrassed, she crossed her arms and looked him straight in the eye. "Mr. Cordell, I do not appreciate such statements in public. I am not here for your amusement." Somehow she'd managed to keep her voice calm. Then she tried to direct her gaze out the window, away from his irresistible eyes.

"Sorry," he pleaded in a more sensitive tone, but there remained a hint of playfulness. "Forgive me?"

She looked at him to acknowledge the apology, but immediately wished she hadn't, for she was captured by his gentler side—the one that made her feel so vulnerable and warm all over. *I can't let him do this to me,* she thought.

"All right. You're forgiven."

"Lucky for me." He smiled, and waved her on to follow him.

"Where are we going?"

"My office. That's where your bag is."

Amanda felt ridiculous for forgetting, but since she'd laid eyes on him she was fighting just to think straight.

Brandon walked up a flight of carpeted stairs and then down a long corridor clearly marked STAFF MEMBERS ONLY. She followed, a little uneasy over being in a restricted area. Finally, he stopped and fished for the proper key. She peered at the door's shiny brass nameplate: B. CORDELL.

Finally the door's lock popped and he held it open for her. Once she passed, he let go of it and it clamped shut, making her jolt at the snap. Being behind closed doors with Brandon didn't settle any easier than being in the hall. So she waited beside the door and leaned against its frame.

From there she surveyed his office, which surprised her—it was nothing close to what she'd imagined from the hallway. A beautiful cherrywood desk and leather swivel-armchair, coupled with other leather armchairs for prospective guests. Behind the scope of his desk, a six-tier bookshelf held numerous volumes and an abundance of tennis paraphernalia. There were plants for decor, and the blinds on the window were opened, revealing a pond outside.

"Here you are." Brandon retrieved her tote bag from a locked cabinet and handed it to her. "My call came through. If you don't mind waiting a moment I'll walk you to your car. I just need to grab a few things."

She realized he was pausing for her approval. *"Make sure he's a gentleman."* Sara's advice flooded her memory. Amanda smiled and nodded.

"You have a substantial office. Are you not telling me something, like you're the chief executive of the club?"

Brandon laughed heartily. "No. They don't treat staff *that* well. Actually, aside from the shelves, this all belongs to me. They originally had some modern, high-tech stuff that I would hesitate to call furniture, so I asked if I could bring my own. It does have drawbacks, though. They told me when I give my resignation I have to leave the furniture." He winked, confirming the joke, then turned to rummage through a stack of papers.

He snatched car keys, paperwork, and a brown, soft-cover book. She recognized it as a galley proof and wondered how he'd obtained it.

"Do you dabble in editing too?" she asked.

"Publishing. Remember the business I mentioned, the one on the side?"

She nodded. "How interesting. My father is a publisher. In fact, that's why we moved here. He bought Huntington House to start on his own."

"Really?" Brandon answered, half continuing his search for things.

He suddenly sounded detached from interest, so Amanda let the subject drop. Viewing his desk, she noticed a small framed picture of Brandon with a dainty, lovely woman. The woman sat on his lap with her arms affectionately slung around his neck. The photo appeared a few years old from the style of the woman's clothes. A lump caught in her throat. With Brandon's comments toward her, she'd always thought of him as unattached. But in light of his good looks and persona, the idea now seemed absurd.

She fidgeted with her tote-bag strap. Curiosity about the woman lingered. "You have a lovely wife," she finally ventured.

Brandon looked up in surprise from his searching. "Huh? Wife?"

She pointed to the picture. His countenance fell. "That's not my wife."

Silence hung between them and Amanda saw the evidence of memories on his face. Dare she ask another question? He seemed a little edgy; it might be better to leave this alone. After all, she wasn't pursuing a relationship with him, so what difference should it make who the lady was?

"There," he said, laying more paperwork inside his briefcase and snapping it shut. Then he guided her out, locking the door behind them.

Amanda reached the lobby and Brandon stopped at the front desk to check for messages. Viewing two paper slips briefly, he slipped them into his shorts pocket. They approached the parking lot and Brandon nodded toward his car. Amanda stopped beside a shiny, black Alfa Romeo, thinking he must have hidden wealth. He placed his briefcase in the passenger seat and closed the door.

"So, you're off to see your paradise?" she asked.

"Yep." He crossed his arms over his chest and leaned against the car door. His biceps rose firmly with the gesture. "Want to come with me?"

Amanda opened her mouth to speak but words abandoned her. She blinked.

Brandon smiled. "You're dying to, Amanda. It's written all over you. Why don't you just say yes?"

She gripped her tote-bag strap and remembered her arrangement for lunch with her father. Swallowing the lump in her throat, she explained, "No, I promised to meet my father for lunch."

"Tomorrow?"

"I have rehearsal."

"Then in a few weeks? Like the Fourth?"

"Pardon? Oh, July Fourth? No, Brandon, I—

"You can't possibly be having rehearsals on a holiday."

"No, but—"

"Be honest. You want to go."

Amanda sighed. She was running out of detours, and his interest wasn't only becoming clear—it was more tempting. He was right about her wanting to go. And he wasn't giving up easily.

"I'll make it worth your while," he said, grinning.

She laughed. "How so?"

"I'll take you to a riding club in Virginia. They're exclusive, the finest in the state. In fact, they're the only one in this state. But you have to be recommended by a member to get in."

"You're a member?"

"And a very close friend of the owner."

Had Brandon offered anything else she wouldn't have considered it further. But he'd found her weak spot and dangled the carrot. His proposal was too enticing and she considered the risk of being alone with him.

"If I visit your cabin, you'll show me this riding club?"

"That's right."

"*And* refer me to the club for membership?"

"Yes. And don't worry, there won't be any problem getting accepted."

She stewed a moment longer and then gave him a tiny smile. "All right, Brandon. I'll come see your paradise."

Chapter Three

The following Saturday Barclay stopped in front of the Faircastle Resort. Feeling a giddy smile creep up on her lips, Amanda hopped out of the BMW and waived him on. As she walked, a string of fireworks crackled in the nearby lot. She yelped from the start and saw a group of young boys scurry away, snickering. She couldn't imagine why Americans set off explosives in celebration. But she also couldn't blame the kids for enjoying themselves. She wanted to try the sparklers herself. And the advertisements for the Charlottesville fireworks show looked fun. Fortunately, there was still a few weeks before the holiday—enough time to convince Sara to go with her.

Amanda scanned the deck, checking faces in the bright sunshine.

Brandon had asked her to meet him at the resort, and

offered to drop her at home on their way back from the cabin.

She glanced each direction. Then she finally saw him, idly leaning against the deck's log railing, not fifteen feet away. Dark sunglasses covered his eyes but it was obvious he was watching her. He grinned from ear to ear, and looked more attractive than ever. *Oh, dear. What have I got myself into?* she silently questioned his frisky smile. White shorts and a sapphire-blue T-shirt accented his dark skin and hair. Amanda took in a steadying breath. As she approached him, Brandon raised the sunglasses to prop upon his head, revealing the seductive glint in his eyes.

"Hello," he greeted her.

"Good morning. I assume you've kept your part of the agreement?"

He handed her a piece of paper and she read the recommendation for membership. "You're in."

Her stomach fluttered. She folded the paper and tucked it in her purse.

"I'm glad you agreed to meet me here. I thought it'd be better to meet here, away from watchful eyes."

"How so? There's at least a dozen people around us."

"But not your father."

Blood heated her face. She recalled her father's questioning her plans this morning in his usual overprotective way. "You're right."

"Thought so," he said, and led the way. They approached the parking lot and he curled his arm around her shoulders. Excitement danced through Amanda. His touch always reached beyond her skin—into her senses. When she'd agreed to come along, she was certain the trip would be free of concerns. Now his suave behavior made her reevaluate things.

Brandon opened the passenger door to help her in. A strange buzzing sound filled her ears. Dizzy spells weren't common to her, so she wondered at her racing heart and why Brandon caused fireworks inside her. She offered a nervous smile when he sat down in the car beside her.

The engine hummed and he backed out, then turned onto the main road.

"Is it a long drive, to your paradise?"

"About two hours."

They drove through town and passed the hill where Monticello sat grandly perched. Brandon pointed out some other popular sites along the way. The mini-tour was welcome. Amanda rarely made it beyond the dance floor. But what made her heart swell was the bountiful land. How wonderful it'd be to own a vast piece of this Virginia acreage and start her stable dream.

Before they left city limits, Brandon stopped to fill the car with gas.

"Would you grab a twenty from my wallet? It's in the glove box."

She popped open the tiny door and retrieved his wallet. Inside, she saw another photo of the woman in his office picture. Her curiosity sparked again. Who was she? Amanda hoped she wasn't spending the day with someone else's boyfriend. She handed him the money and replaced his wallet while he paid.

Back on their way, she drummed her fingers on her knee. Her interest was piqued and she couldn't help mentioning the woman again.

"Brandon?" she ventured.

"Yes?"

"I know this is a rather personal question, but . . . who is the lady?"

His smile melted. "My kid sister, Jeannie." His hands clenched around the steering wheel.

"*Kid* sister?" Unexpectedly relieved, she ventured further. "She looked rather grown up. How old is she now?"

He stiffened. "She isn't. She died the year the picture was taken."

Amanda saw hurt and rage cross his face and she felt nauseated. "I am so sorry. I didn't realize. I—"

"It's all right," he broke her string of apologies. "You couldn't have known." He turned to meet her eyes and sighed heavily. "My sister was murdered nine years ago. We went to dinner one night to celebrate her promotion. As we walked back to the car there was a gunshot. I turned to protect Jeannie—it was too late." His face grew stern. "I miss her."

Amanda was stunned by his private suffering. She noticed a glistening in his eyes. Keeping silent, she wished she hadn't been intrusive.

"Jeannie and I were very close," he said.

"Brandon . . . why did they—?"

"Simple mistake. They were supposed to hit me, but they missed."

The word *me* shot through her mind as loud and fast as the gunshot she imagined. Why did someone want to kill him? Were they still looking for him? Her chest constricted, shortening her breath.

She wanted to inquire further, but sensing his despair

she retreated. It was best to wait, let him tell the story when he was ready.

The sunlight's warmth was physically soothing. Amanda leaned back to resume watching the scenery and wishing for a stretch of it to call her own.

The car rolled to a stop. Amanda woke to blinding sunlight.

"Tough rehearsals this week?" Brandon asked, brushing a wisp of fallen hair from her sun-warmed face.

"Always." The sun's radiance hurt her eyes, making her squint. "What time is it? Are we there?" Slowly, bushy green trees came into focus. They surrounded most of the cabin at the end of the road.

"Almost noon." He smiled, watching her. "And we are roughly fifty miles southwest of Charlottesville, tucked away in the beautiful Blue Ridge highlands. This is my paradise."

His voice was gentle. It soothed her. She needed some serenity in her life. Brandon slid out of the car and came around to open her door.

"Come on. I can't wait to show you the place."

Amanda swung her sneakered feet outside and accepted his hand for assistance. As she slid forward, she saw her legs become displayed by the hiked summer skirt. She also noticed his grin. Her pulse escalated, and she quickly stood, smoothing down her skirt.

Brandon unlocked the cabin door and pushed it in a few inches. "Ladies first." He gestured a slight bow and waited for her to walk through.

Amanda opened the door the rest of the way and halted in her steps, seeing straight through the foyer and out several picture windows that spanned the face of the house. "Wow!" she said, and walked through the clean, homey interior to get a closer look at the view. A hilly ravine, dotted with dogwood and elm trees, extended beyond the manicured front lawn. But the Blue Ridge mountains were clearly the paramount sight. She gazed at the distant crests and valleys, draped in velvety shades of green, blue, and violet.

She was speechless, fascinated by the panoramic beauty beyond the glass wall, and lost in its splendor.

"It's so beautiful, Brandon."

"I knew you'd like it."

"Like it? It's spectacular! You built this cabin?"

"Well, I had a few friends to help, but the plans were mine. Only the foundation from my father's cabin is original. The rest is new."

She heard the clink of car keys upon the glass coffee table. Then she felt him walk up behind her. He stood so close that Amanda tensed. She could feel his warm breath behind her ear. Then he slipped a hand underneath her hair and pulled it off to one side. The heat in his fingertips glided across her neck, making her skin tingle. She held her breath.

"Your hair is so beautiful. Like black silk."

Swallowing, she tried to sound casual. "Thanks. It's usually kept in a braid for rehearsals." She turned slowly and looked up into Brandon's blue eyes. The attraction she felt for him was impossible to deny, but she knew it was wise to keep some distance between them and she stepped backward.

His eyes sparkled and he reached for her hand. "Come on," he said. "There's something else you have to see."

Pulling her away from the superb panorama he led her outside, beyond the wooden deck and onto a beaten trail. They hiked down a deep ravine, across a creek, and started upward again, climbing a narrow path in the steep, wooded hill. The whole way, Brandon brushed off her questions about where they were going. Finally Amanda begged him to stop, needing to catch her breath.

"We're almost there." He pointed in front of him. "Look, see that huge rock in front of us? There's a ledge there."

"This better be good," she muttered, inhaling deeply and taking a few slow steps. She wondered what was worth such a long, exacting trek, causing her leg muscles to tighten worse than dancing.

Brandon climbed onto the ledge and disappeared beyond her line of vision. She marched a few more strides and pulled herself up onto the massive, flat stone. Out of breath and in awe, she sat beside him on the cool surface to rest. "Unbelievable," she whispered, scarcely able to talk.

"There's no place in Virginia that compares to this."

"I should say . . . not in the world." Amanda saw the cabin nestled thickly in the woods, a fair distance across the ravine. The creek they'd crossed lay hundreds of feet below, winding out a miniature scalloped pattern.

"Look!" Brandon pointed and Amanda looked beyond his finger. She smiled. A mother deer grazed with her fawn less than thirty yards away. The peaceful creatures seemed unconcerned about the closeness of humans.

"This *is* paradise," she breathed her praise.

"This is home," he replied, leaning back against the

shaded, slanted rock behind him. He laced his fingers behind his head. "I can't help but love it here. I've made plans to move in as soon as it can be arranged."

"Little wonder. Such beauty is rather hypnotic."

"The place was left to me when my father passed away a couple of years ago. The old cabin was pitiful. I could never understand why someone as filthy rich as my father would live in such a ridiculous, unattractive heap." He laughed heartily and an echo resounded through the ravine. "So I rebuilt it."

She was watching him and he turned, meeting her gaze.

"It's all mine, Amanda—as far as the mountain foot-hills." Brandon looked again at the vast, deciduous land. "About six miles square."

"My gracious! You can't mean . . . *all* of this belongs to you?"

"Yep. Well, except the deer and animals." He winked.

"You're so fortunate. What will you do with it?"

"I've thought of a few options, but nothing definite— except that I'm not selling any of it. I want my kids to have it."

"It's too beautiful to let go of."

"Yes." His voice sounded husky, serious. "A lot like you."

Amanda looked at him. The butterflies returned in her stomach. She knew she needed to change the subject or her feelings would be influenced.

"Tell me about Jeannie. What was she like?"

He plucked a nearby flower and twirled it around, concentrating on it. "She was loving, fun, beautiful, and very honest. She always let me know where I stood, even though I was older. In high school, our favorite pastime was going to basketball games and then out for pizza. We had a bunch of the same friends, which made it easy to spend time together. But I think it was also because we enjoyed each other's company. I suppose we still fought like siblings, but I can't remember many of those times. When I lost Jeannie, I lost more of a friend than a family member.''

Brandon grimaced. Amanda was touched by the knowledge of his sister.

''I suppose it's different for you, since you're an only child.''

''Yes, but when I was younger, in senior school, my closest friends were sisters in a large family. I became an adopted daughter of sorts. We often had sleep-overs, until Mother died. Then it was harder to leave Father.''

''How did she die?''

''Leukemia. It was so very quick—four months after she was diagnosed.''

''I'm sorry. It's a terrible pain to lose a loved one.''

She nodded, accepting his empathy. ''Sara, our housekeeper, and I became very close afterward. But nothing fills the emptiness of losing your mother.''

Brandon offered a tender, understanding smile.

Amanda brought her knees up to one side. ''My mother was always so positive. She encouraged me to never lose hope for my dreams.'' Amanda sighed, grateful for the special moments with her mother.

''And have you?''

''Lost hope? Sometimes, but not completely, not when I remember her.''

Amanda pushed her bangs from her face. Feeling a tiny dogwood branch caught in her hair, she loosened it and combed the ebony waves with her fingers. As she pulled her hair to one side she realized Brandon was watching her. His expression showed a mixture of anguish and delight.

"I'm hungry," he said, standing and dusting himself off. "What do you say we head back for lunch?"

Brandon carefully lifted her, protecting her from the edge. As she stood beside him they simply watched each other. Amanda sensed a powerful lure between them. Then he let loose of her hands and reached for her waist, gently pulling her toward him. His fingers traced up and down her bare arms, leaving a tingling in their wake. He lifted a hand and caressed the soft pad of her cheek. She closed her eyes, feeling the quickening thump of her heartbeat. *Please.* Every fiber in her ached for his kiss.

Slowly, he bent forward, kissing her so gently. She reached up to place her hands around his head. Brandon curled his arms around her and pulled her tighter toward him. His warmth caused a current to race through her, and she battled a fervent hunger for more.

He glided his lips over to her ear, brushing her earlobe. Then he planted a few kisses on her neck. She felt herself melting in his arms.

"Amanda . . ." He buried his face in her hair, hugging her tightly. His chest expanded against hers and he pulled back, revealing an eagerness in his smile. "Now, about that lunch, before my appetite loses control."

Adrenaline surged through her head, making her ears buzz. She tried to clear her throat. "Good idea."

As they started down the trail Brandon reached for her hand and she accepted it around hers.

After having BLTs, Brandon gave Amanda a tour through the rest of the cabin, passing up only the master bedroom. She listened as he explained his design plans and how the construction had been done.

After the tour, he challenged her to a game of cribbage. One game led to another, and after an hour they finished up with a tiebreaker. Winning the game, Brandon stood to stretch.

"I should have picked up some fireworks," he said. "It'll be dark in a few hours."

Amanda suddenly realized how far west the sun had migrated. "Oh, no! What time is it?"

"Going on six. What's the rush?"

"It's getting too late. I have to get back."

He approached her chair from behind and leaned over her, nuzzling her ear. "But Cinderella, my car doesn't turn into a pumpkin until midnight."

Amanda quickly hopped out of the chair, turning around to look at him. "Please understand. I told my father I'd be sight-seeing today. He'll be worried soon, and upset."

Brandon looked sober. "Of course," he said, and walked over to stare out the window. He shook his head. "One thing's for sure." His voice carried a bitter tone. "Jonathan Chambers won't approve of my seeing you."

His bold statement puzzled her, and she went over to him. The stark look on his face caused apprehension to prickle through her. She lifted an eyebrow. "You keep calling my father by name. How do you know him, Brandon? Through your publishing?"

He turned to face her and in his eyes she saw a fragment of pain.

"Yeah. I know him. You're bound to run into other publishers in this business." He shook his head and gave a short, cynical laugh. "Your father took an instant disliking to me."

"When? What happened?"

"I met him last year at Jillian's Books in London. The second time we met was this morning. I went to Huntington House to see if we could reconcile our differences, but he kicked me out. Even told me he'd have me arrested if I came around again." Brandon's expression changed, becoming devoid of emotion. "Truthfully, he could care less about *really* knowing me."

"What does that mean?"

"It means he's conjured up something against me in his mind, and he's not willing to let go of it, no matter how irrational it is." Brandon paused, drawing in a weighty breath. "I suggest you keep him from knowing the truth, unless you want him to cut off our relationship—and he *will* put a stop to it, Amanda." His frank stare matched the bluntness of his words.

Relationship? The idea raised questions in her mind. What relationship? Then Amanda suddenly realized the impact of his suggestion. "If you're suggesting that I live a lie, that is out of the question! I have a very loyal and honest relationship with my father."

"You're very loyal, but not so honest. You've been hiding something from him for most of your life, and you know it."

"That's absurd."

"Is it, now?" He peered at her mockingly. "Come

on, Amanda. Admit it. *He's* the reason you haven't followed your deepest desire in life. Even a stranger can
see that you'd rather be working with horses than re-
hearsing ballet. So why doesn't your father know, if
you're so honest with him?''

''You've no right to tell me how to conduct my life.''

''Neither does he. You're a grown woman. You need
to stop letting him treat you like Daddy's little girl!''

Amanda's anger flared. She clenched her shaking fists
and tucked them tightly under her arms, turning away.

''I'm sorry, Amanda. But . . . you know it's true.''

His gentler tone made her throat tighten and she felt
the stinging of tears behind her eyes. She kept her back
to him in silence.

''I'll wait in the car,'' Brandon said, and plucked his
car keys from the table. He flipped off the lights, leaving
her in the partially lit room.

Amanda swallowed at the lump in her throat. She tried
to hold her escalating hurt in check. Then she shook her
head as she admitted the truth: she had to end this
wretched pretending. It was time to take a stand.

Silence choked the air during their drive back to Charlottesville. They skipped visiting the stables altogether,
but as far as Amanda was concerned it was for the best.
She had the information anyway.

Brandon stopped at the edge of her driveway and let
her off beside the tall hedges, as she requested.

''Good night. Thank you.'' She opted for a quick fare-
well.

In the car's dome light, Amanda saw his knuckles
were white from gripping the gearshift. He nodded,

keeping his gaze upon the road ahead. She closed the door and turned to walk home as the car roared off.

Amanda faced the long driveway. It stretched almost one-quarter mile to her father's estate, winding up the luxurious grassland. Yet before she faced her father she needed time to think. She began the promenade, sorting out her feelings as she shuffled her tennis shoes along the gravel road.

Approaching the house, she saw its silhouette framed by the sunset. It looked so peaceful. How could so much family turmoil exist there? Not at all enjoying the thought of hiding things from her father, she resigned to a sight-seeing story and reminded herself that considering the circumstances, it was the best for all concerned.

"One day, Amanda . . . one day," she muttered, and quickened her steps to the house, prepared to face the inquisitions she knew awaited her.

Entering, she glanced around. Barclay, in his other role as handyman, was changing chandelier bulbs and immediately spotted her as she closed the door.

"Land sakes, Amanda! It's almost nine o'clock. Your father's worried."

Barclay's chastening made her even more jumpy and she wished she'd at least called. "The time just got away from me. Is Daddy still up, Barclay?"

"I'll say he is, and he's waiting for you, as well. In the den. Now go let him know you're alive." He flailed a hand in the direction of the den—the only place her father went when something troubled him.

From down the hall light shafted through a cracked opening in the doorway, casting a golden beam against the wall. She knocked.

"Come in!"

With his abrupt reply she peeked through the doorway, swallowing to clear her throat. "You asked to see me?"

"Amanda! Where've you been? We've been expecting you since dinner!" He stood, color entering his cheeks in splotches. His eyes showed worry.

She blinked. His anger weakened her resolve. Jonathan Chambers was often too protective, but he wasn't a man given to heated displays of emotion.

"Yes, I-I'm sorry. I should have telephoned."

"I have been sick not hearing from you. And it's now dark!" Jonathan removed his reading glasses and tossed them onto the desk.

"Yes, I know . . . I just wanted to do some sight-seeing around town. I left word with Barclay this morning that I would be out for the day."

"And half the night, I might add. How did you get home, anyway?"

"The club's tour guide gave me a ride." Her stomach knotted at the fragmented truth, and she tried to ignore her queasiness.

"Humph," he grumbled, surveying her from head to toe.

Amanda felt like a child forgetting to look both ways before crossing the street. She was inches to telling him it was none of his business, but his expression finally softened and his cheeks resumed a normal color.

"Well, you are an adult. I apologize for overreacting, darling. I was concerned for your safety."

The distress on his face intensified. Guilt started to claw at Amanda's insides. "No, I should have been more considerate."

Jonathan stared at the floor for a moment. "Enough about that. There's something else I need to discuss with you."

He moved in front of the desk and leaned against it, picking up the glasses again to fidget with. A nervous habit, she recalled.

"Yes?" She waited while he grappled with his thoughts.

"Initially, I was very pleased to become the owner of this publishing house. However, today I ran into someone I once met in England a year ago."

Jonathan turned to stare at the bookshelves and Amanda's heartbeat launched into double time. Brandon? She fought her rising nausea.

"This lad is a writer. I don't know much about him, but I have heard that he doesn't know where to draw the line in writers' ethics. There are private things you simply shouldn't print about other people's livelihoods." He faced her squarely, smokey-gray eyes revealing his anguish.

Amanda thought she would faint. She knew well who he was referring to and she braced herself to hear what Brandon had kept secret at the cabin.

Chapter Four

Amanda reached the top of the stairs. *How could I be so foolish?* she scolded herself. She flung her bedroom door shut and paced beside the moonlit bay window, not bothering to turn on the light. *Trusting a mere stranger. Spending the day alone with him.* She was amazed at her own naïveté.

Derrek Madison. She wondered at the name her father had mentioned. An assumed name. How many enemies did this man have, anyway?

Her mind replayed the conversation with her father.

"Who's life is he writing about?" she'd asked.

"That's not important. What matters is that he's compiling a new book with information that could ruin someone if it was printed. Since I know who the book is about, this writer wanted me to do the book's foreword, to support it. I told him that I would never condone this book. But he had the nerve to threaten me with consequences if I didn't help expose this man.''

''Threaten you?'' Amanda had paled at the mental pictures in her mind. She'd felt her stomach wrench, instantly alarmed that she'd kissed a potentially dangerous man. ''He means you harm?''

''That's precisely why I'm informing you. I've told Barclay and Sara as well. He'll take advantage of anyone just to sell another book, the jackal! I want you to be aware of who this character is, Amanda. His name is Derrek Madison. If he comes around I'll have the authorities arrest him.''

Her father went on but the name had seized Amanda's concentration.

Now she stared at the blackened night. This new information made it clear that she shouldn't have any further contact with Brandon. Or was it Derrek? One thing was sure, her father was unaware of Brandon's new name and life in Virginia, and Amanda decided *not* to be the one to fill him in.

Her mind hummed with questions. She wanted answers. She couldn't get them from her father, so that left one person. But that would mean seeing Brandon again, and she wasn't sure that was such a good idea . . . not after the way he'd kissed her.

Amanda strode through the front door, relieved the week of rehearsal was finally over. She passed Barclay in his room, reading. Then she made her way into the kitchen, spying a note from Sara about running into town. Her father would be home any minute. Friday was bank errand day, leaving Jonathan's assistant, Benjamin, to close the small publishing house.

Too hungry to wait for Sara's return, Amanda made some soup and rolls. As she finished setting the table, Jonathan strode through the kitchen door.

"Hello, dear. How was rehearsal?" he asked, sitting down at the table.

"Strenuous. I don't know how I'll make it through summer preparation. My legs ache." She placed his bowl of soup down, suddenly remembering her long trek with Brandon. That had gotten her week off to a sore start.

Jonathan only chuckled. "Stay fit for those auditions, and you'll soon be the company's new prima ballerina."

Amanda set the platter of rolls down a little too firmly and one bounced off the plate. She replaced it, pursing her lips at her father's enthusiasm. His obsession with her success at ballet always made her resentful.

"Daddy, I don't intend to be the best."

Jonathan looked surprised at her answer. "Don't be modest. I've seen you dance. You are part of the company's pride."

How could she abhor something and still be so good at it? She knew her performance over the years was excellent, but it was utterly ironic—the more she disliked rehearsals, the more passion she poured into her dancing.

Returning to familiar silence, they ate their meal. Jonathan sipped his Earl Grey tea, adding some milk. Amanda watched the creamy white liquid swirl into a sandy color. The grandfather clock ticked away. She tensed. Their private moment was a perfect time to talk to him about riding.

"Did you know there's a private riding club only a few miles away? I've been thinking of riding again." She faced her teacup and took a long sip, finally looking up to meet her father's eyes. His scrunched face and squarely set jaw showed his reservation. But she was determined to sit this one out. It was a meager start, but at least she'd said the words.

Frowning and breathing faster, Jonathan cleared his throat and planted both elbows on the table, lacing his fingers together. More silence. She wondered if he would answer her at all.

"There's still several hours of sunlight," she continued. "I'd like to go tonight, if you didn't have any . . . objections." She imagined the fiery protests in his mind, but she waited as the silence hung between them.

Finally, he picked up his spoon again and looked down at his meal. "All right, Amanda. Yes. I say, it's been a long time."

His words lit a furnace of hope inside of her. She stared, unbelieving. His frown was removed but grooves of concern were still deeply set.

"Really?" She smiled, amazed.

"I'll drop you off and pick you up again at eight-thirty. It should be close to dusk then."

"I can drive. There's no need to—"

"It's no problem, Amanda."

As frustrating as it was to be carted around at her age, she didn't want to jeopardize the progress she'd just made by arguing. She sucked in a deep breath. "I'll change right away," she answered, clearing the dishes.

Amanda raced up the stairway to her room and retrieved her riding clothes from their treasured spot. She hoped they still fit. Luckily, her figure hadn't changed too much since her teen years, and the outfit was only a bit snug in certain places. She hurried back down the stairs, nearly colliding with Sara as they came around the same corner at the base.

"Oh!" Sara raised her hand to her heart, then noticed Amanda's clothes. "Amanda! You're dressed for riding?"

"Daddy's taking me now. Can you believe it?" she whispered.

Sara smiled and hugged her. "I'm so glad. You'll be home before dark?"

"Yes. He's picking me up at eight-thirty." Amanda turned and left.

The drive to Hargreaves' Stables took only twenty-five minutes, but to Amanda it seemed like hours. Jonathan pulled the BMW in front of the riding club office, and she pressed the door handle.

He reached for her shoulder, and she looked his way. "How did you hear of this place?"

She felt the blood drain from her face. "At the club."

He nodded pensively. "See you at half past eight. Please, be timely."

His thin face was now grooved with concern. It pained her to see him this way. Although she loathed his sheltering manner, she never forgot how he and her mother had spent every night with her at the hospital. It was probably difficult for him to let go.

"I will." She kissed his cheek and stepped out of the car.

Carrying her black hat, Amanda walked in the stable office and glanced eagerly for the clerk. Only a couple of people were in the room. She noticed a redheaded, heavyset man sitting at a table by the front counter, a folded newspaper in one hand and a steaming mug in the other.

"Excuse me, sir. I'm looking for the desk clerk."

The man looked up from his coffee. His graying, carrot-colored eyebrows were equally as bright as his hair. "Why, that'd be me, little lady." He examined her from head to toe, offering a friendly smile that was barely visible between his mustache and beard.

She smiled. "I've been referred for membership. May I sign?"

"Say, that's some potent accent you got there." He left his coffee and strode over to the countertop to root out a clipboard and some papers. He placed them in front of her. "What're you dressed up for? Don't have much competition 'round here."

Amanda realized he meant her clothes, and her cheeks grew warm. "I—these are my only riding clothes. You don't require them, traditionally?"

"No, not traditionally. He winked a soft gray eye, mimicking her sweetly. "But I must say, you look mighty fine in 'em so you should wear 'em here anytime you like."

"Thank you."

"What's your name?"

"Amanda Chambers."

"And who referred you?"

"Mr. Brandon Cordell. He contacted the stables a few days ago."

The man hummed as he perused another clipboard of

paperwork. "Yep. Here you are. We only provide membership on a monthly basis."

"That's fine. How much is the fee?"

"That'll be one hundred fifty dollars. And we've got some rules you should read over first, here. But the only ones important to me are that you're nice to our horses and bring 'em back before dark. The ponies gotta eat, you know."

She smiled, amused by his language. For such an exclusive, fancy riding club, this eccentric and kind man seemed very down-to-earth. She imagined him hustling cattle and slapping the dust off of cowboy boots.

She pulled three fifty-dollar bills from her small leather purse and handed them to him. "Thank you, Mr., umm . . ."

"Finley. Sam Finley."

"Are you the owner?"

"No. That's Ms. Hargreaves. She ain't here right now. I work the evenin' shift and weekends. Ms. Hargreaves works the weekdays till five." He smiled again, crinkling his middle-aged, sun-reddened face. "Say, where you from anyway? Anyone could tell you're English."

"London. My father and I moved to Charlottesville two months ago."

"London, eh?"

"And how long have you lived here, Mr. Finley?"

" 'Bout a year, myself. Got this job through a friend who lives in Virginia. Used to own a cattle ranch in Texas, but I grew tired of it, sold the lot, and decided to try my hand at ponies for a while."

Amanda smiled.

He handed her copies of all the paperwork and walked

into the back room, emerging a minute later with his arms full of paraphernalia. "Here's your tack, and since you're new I'll show you to the stables."

Finley led her outside and down a sloped trail. Beyond the thicket of bushes there were thirty-some stables, complete with riding rings and walkers.

Amanda stopped. The small hairs tingled on the nape of her neck as she caught sight of the horses poking their heads out of most of the stalls. Her eyes misted with unshed tears. "This is so . . . wonderful," she whispered.

"Which one do you like?"

"Which?" Amanda laughed, feeling nervous and elated all at once. "I haven't any idea. Would you recommend one that might like me?"

"Sure." They walked again. "Let's see . . . how about Brittany? Since you're English and all?" Chuckling at his own joke, he led her over to a sleek, tall, charcoal-black Arabian. Amanda patted the mare's soft muzzle and smoothed her hand down its long, velvety neck. Sam strapped on the saddle and bridle, then looked to Amanda. "Like her?"

"She's beautiful. Should I know about any special tricks of hers?"

"Oh! You should at that. Brittany used to be a race-horse. If you whistle softly in her ears she runs like the wind. Uncontrollable! Had an awful time stoppin' her myself once. Well, have fun. Remember to be back before dark. The ponies gotta—"

"Yes, they need to eat." She laughed. "Don't worry. I'll be back before then." Amanda mounted, then clicked her tongue and the mare started off in an effortless trot.

There were several rings to use but the open acreage

was all that interested Amanda. She left the trail for the pastures, posting to the steady cadence of Brittany's trot. The horse moved smoothly, in perfect rhythm.

Amanda sighed amid the beautiful leafy trees, small bushes, and grassland. She wished the moment could be endless. She led Brittany through a tiny stream and saw a large stretch beyond the pasture that led gradually up a long hill. The countryside was barren of other riders, so she decided this was an ideal, private place.

"Well, Brittany. Let's see what kind of steam you have." She leaned forward and whistled softly in the animal's fluffy ears.

The mare's body stiffened and it bolted off, reaching an incredible speed in seconds. Oddly enough, the farther she climbed the slope, the faster she ran. Amanda couldn't contain her squeal, reveling in the thrill. The hoofbeats thundered faster and faster, pounding away years of her agony with every gallop.

They neared the top of the hill and Amanda looked for the descending pasture—but saw only a cliff dropping beyond the hill's crest.

"Whoa!" She pulled the reins, trying to halt the mare's racing. But Brittany had no intention of slowing. "Whoa, Brittany!" Amanda gave two more grueling tugs, to no avail. The horse barreled toward the cliff's edge. Fear sprang into Amanda's heart.

"Whooaa!" she screamed.

The black beast skidded and stopped abruptly at the edge, nostrils flaring. Amanda's scream echoed into the valley below. She gasped for breath, blinking and staring dizzily at the plummeting ridge only five feet in front of her. She dismounted to let the two of them catch their breath, wishing she'd asked Mr. Finley the secret to stopping Brittany as well.

Amanda collapsed on the warm grass to calm her racing heart. Her ears still drummed with pounding hoofbeats, but she suddenly realized that they got louder. She sat up to see if Finley had followed her. But it wasn't Sam.

"Brandon," she whispered. A flicker of last night's anger reignited, and she returned her stare to the scenery, drawing up her knees to wrap her arms around them. His buckskin horse trotted up beside Brittany. The two beasts eagerly sniffed noses as Brandon dismounted. He carried her hat and held it out to her. He was as alluring as ever, but his eyes hinted at anxiety. He looked her over.

"You okay?"

"Yes, thank you," she answered coldly, taking the hat to set it down.

"I see you've made progress with your father."

She returned her gaze to the valley. "How convenient that we'd both be riding at this hour." She tried to act indifferent, but his blue eyes had already begun melting her resolve.

"All right. I confess I spoke with Sara. My call just missed you at the house, so I left immediately to try to catch you here. When Sam said you'd just left with Brittany, I knew it would be wise to follow you. She has a serious knack for kicking up her heels if you—"

"—whistle softly in her ears, yes, I know."

"So you've been told. The only thing to do is wear her out. She's the best mare in this state, that I know of." He walked over to the cliff's edge and examined the descent. "That's quite a drop. You had me concerned. I knew Raydon wouldn't be able to catch up to Brittany.'' He patted the sturdy gelding on the back.

"I'll thank you not to waste your concerns on me, Mr. Cordell.''

Brandon walked directly in front of her and stood in her line of vision. She tried to see beyond him but his intense gaze chipped away her resentment. She sighed, and finally looked at him. "Would you at least move aside?''

"Sure.'' He approached her and dropped to the ground, lying next to her.

She wished he wasn't so close. She tightened her hold around her knees. She could feel his gaze still fixed upon her.

"I thought we were on a first-name basis,'' he ventured.

"That was before. Things have changed.''

"Before what?''

"Before I found out the person you pretend to be is not you at all.''

"Look,'' he began apologetically, "I apologize for last night, for being brusque . . . I was wrong. I'm sorry.''

He waited. Amanda caught the scent of his spicy aftershave in the mild breeze, but her heart was still frozen. Now she knew about the impact of his books on others' lives, about his profiting at the exposure of another's mistakes.

"Amanda, will you forgive me?'' He rested his large hand upon hers. The warmth of his palm began melting her icy feelings. But she still needed answers. Knowing she didn't have the strength to ignore him, she proposed to answer him, but keep her emotions—and her lips—at a distance.

"This time," she said, and turned to look at him.

"Thank you." His countenance softened and he returned a tender smile. He was clean-shaven, clad in worn jeans. His white cotton shirt was loosely tucked in. The sleeves had been rolled to his elbows and tiny, light-brown hairs curled across his forearms. His top shirt buttons were left unfastened, leaving his chest partially exposed . . . and too appealing. She looked away.

Brandon reached to twirl a portion of her hair between his fingers. Then he stroked the soft pillow of her cheek with his hand. She quivered at his gentleness. No, this would only complicate things.

"B-Brandon, I'm not comfortable with seeing you. I think—"

"Amanda . . ." He caressed her neck and stared at her with a look of building desire. "There isn't anything I want besides you."

She swallowed. Her pulse accelerated as emotions traitorously responded to his caress. She felt herself abandoning her former resolve to keep distance between them.

"Don't you see how much I want to be with you?" he whispered.

Amanda closed her eyes, steeling herself against the beckoning in his voice. "Yes, but I *can't* see you."

He reached softly to trace her lips with his finger. "It's not my intention merely to see you, Amanda."

She opened her eyes again to look at him. *Don't. Don't do this to me. I want answers,* she thought.

"You're ravishing. Is everything about you soft and

smooth?'' he whispered, leaning closer to brush his lips against her neck. The contact awakened every nerve in her body. Then he kissed her lips. Cupping her head he pulled her closer, kissing more eagerly. The feel of his strong arms and warm kiss made her head spin, and all her thoughts faded into one ache for his touch.

Amanda's mind flashed with the memory of her father's anger. Reasoning returned and she suddenly pushed away, making an effort to halt her madness.

Brandon observed her curiously. ''What?''

Pulling her thoughts together, she moved away. ''This is absurd,'' she spoke with deliberation. ''I can't let you do this to me.''

''What do I do to you?'' He grinned and propped himself up on one arm.

Amanda's lips felt tingly and hot from his kisses, but she persisted. ''I won't let you ruin my life like you've ruined others.'' She thrust the accusation at him, wishing the knowledge of his past would disappear.

''What others? There are no others.'' He sat upright and glared at her. ''What are you talking about?''

''I'm referring to your former life. Your reputation followed you.''

''Reputation? I'm the person you see me to be.''

''And just how well do you suppose that I know you, *'Brandon'?*''

''I suppose there's plenty of things you haven't had time to learn, but we can fix that. What's the problem, Amanda?''

She stood to her feet to confront him. ''*Who* you are, Brandon, is precisely the problem. Or is your real name Derrek Madison? Remember?''

He stared in silence. She crossed her arms, anticipating a shameful explanation, but he offered none. Instead, he stood and stepped toward her.

"Amanda, what you feel for me is right. I know you know that, so why don't you start listening to your heart and stop listening to your father?"

His truth pierced her logic, but she wasn't going to admit it. "Because he's my father. I've known him for twenty-three years. *You* are merely a stranger—someone who hides his past."

"That can be changed."

"I doubt it. You're probably pretending to care for me just to get something from my father. How could you threaten him?"

"That's insane!" His raised voice echoed into the valley. "I told you from the beginning that your father held an aversion to me for some unknown reason. But I've never set out to hurt anyone. Nor would I."

"No? Then why did you publish those awful books, wrecking the lives of so many people?"

"What?" A puzzled look crossed his face, but Amanda didn't want to be tricked into believing any excuses.

"I don't want anything to do with you," she blurted, and whirled around to mount Brittany.

"You're mistaken. Amanda—wait!"

She grabbed the reins and faced him. "My only mistake was letting you kiss me!" She kicked and whistled for Brittany to take flight. The rested animal sprang into action and pounded down the slope. Amanda's eyes burned hot with restrained tears. One tear escaped, streaking her cheek sideways in the wind. She managed to curb Brittany this time, and they angled off into a wooded area. Amanda dismounted to sit at the trunk of a tree. There she released her guarded heart, allowing it to crumble as her sobs broke through.

The weeping spell subsided and she remained at the tree a while, waiting for her vision to clear. Finally she mounted Brittany and rode into another pasture. She spent the remainder of her ride speculating over Brandon's plea. "You're mistaken," he'd said. Could she be? she wondered. She hadn't given him a chance to explain. What if there was something she wasn't aware of?

She glanced at her watch, remembering the passing time. Eight-fifteen. Thank goodness she wasn't late. But it was time to head back, so she turned Brittany around to head for the stables. Approaching the stalls she swung down and led the mare into her stall. Amanda removed the tack and came around to close the stall door. She placed the tack on a nearby sawhorse, then leaned on the gate to pet Brittany, disheartened by the impending separation.

"Wish you were mine," she cooed. Brittany rested her muzzle in Amanda's hand, flapping her fuzzy lips in a show of hunger.

"Wishes can come true, you know."

Amanda flinched and turned to see Finley behind her. She sighed. "I would trade the world for a chance at life with her."

"Yeah, she's a beauty. Been my favorite. Gonna hate to see her go."

Amanda straightened. "Go? You can't mean she's leaving?"

" 'Fraid so. Brittany *and* the whole business is goin'

up for sale," he confided, nodding. "That's why our memberships are now monthly."

"But why?"

"Well, it seems a personal decision of Ms. Hargreaves. Business reasons, she claims. She's contracted to sell this land to a developer. Imagine, all this will be turned into a golf course and condos in two years. The horses are going to auction at the end of summer. If they weren't so expensive, I'd buy the lot of 'em. These ponies have become my friends."

As if on cue, Brittany shifted over to Finley and nuzzled her black nose into his neck. The twosome shared a tender moment, like old buddies. Finley pulled his handkerchief to dab his eyes.

"That's dreadful," Amanda remarked. His tale extinguished her hope of riding much longer. This was the only stable around for miles.

"Well . . ." He blew his nose, and shoved the hankie back into his pocket. "It's feeding time. I better get ready to do rounds."

"I'll need to leave as well."

Amanda walked back up the hill to the parking lot. Now, even more so, she wanted to confront her father about her longtime dream of operating her own stables. She decided to explain her hopes and plans to him, no matter what the outcome. It wouldn't be easy. Confronting Jonathan Chambers required lots of backbone and that elusive "perfect timing."

Parked in the front lot was her father's silver BMW, and inside sat Barclay, no doubt asked to do the honors. As she opened the car door she glimpsed Brandon. He sat upon a partially unearthed boulder, less than twenty feet away, observing her. His earnest gaze salted her wound. After a brief hesitation, she slumped inside the car and slammed the door shut.

Amanda stewed during the ride home. Talking to her father wasn't the only challenge before her. She also had to cancel her tennis lessons. After all, the stable idea was her real hope for independence, and she couldn't risk losing her dream because of the charms of one attractive man.

Chapter Five

Amanda walked into the living room. Her father sat in his favorite wing chair, reading the newspaper. He acknowledged her with a smile and refolded the paper to a new section. He seemed cheerful. Maybe now was the time.

"Hello, dear. How was your ride?" He peeked over his glasses.

"Wonderful." Amanda sat in the jade velour chair beside him and crossed her legs to appear relaxed. "There's something I'd like to discuss with you. I've been thinking about an idea for a long time."

He set down the paper and removed his glasses. "What's on your mind?"

Jonathan returned to his usual reserved air, and it reminded her why she never found it easy to be bold around him.

"Well, I heard that Hargreaves' Stables is going out of business."

"Hmm. How did you find this out?"

"From the attendant. He's not the owner, but he explained they are going to auction all of the horses at the end of summer. And . . . well, I—"

"What's your point, Amanda?" Her father's demeanor grew more austere.

"I'd like to purchase some of the thoroughbreds, one mare in particular, and possibly four others to open up my own riding business. We have plenty of acreage to build a small business. I'd lease the land from you, of course."

"How do you intend to accomplish such a venture? Purebreds cost thousands of dollars apiece, not to mention business start-up expenses."

She straightened in the chair and whisked in a quick breath. "I'd like to use the remainder of Mother's endowment."

"You can't be serious!" he protested. "Those funds are yours for ballet. I won't have you squandering it on some ridiculous purchase." He paused for air. "Listen to what you're saying, Amanda. That money should be used wisely or invested, not carelessly splurged. You can't pour it into something that can go bankrupt tomorrow, just to suit your fancy. They're selling out. Doesn't that tell you something about the risks involved?"

"*Not* from lack of funds. The owner is selling to make a profit on the land, not because of a failure of the stable business. Daddy, you forget that I minored in business. I never told you, but I spent two years studying and planning for this. My term final was the preparation of an outline of operations for a stable business, with blueprints, sketches, and a proposal for expenditures. My professor asked permission to use it in future classes as an example of an intelligent business stratagem.''

He looked at her in shock, having never learned of the news before now. Amanda never had the courage to tell him about her enterprising idea and the resounding praise it had received from her college professor.

''Besides, this is a spectacular career opportunity.'' She was surprised at the strength in her voice.

''Your career is in ballet,'' Jonathan boomed. ''Now please stop this nonsensical conversation.''

Amanda tensed. Her endurance had reached its limit. ''Ballet is *your* career, Daddy! *You* chose it for me. I've never exercised any choice in the matter, except to try my best at it, which I have. But I can't keep hiding my feelings just to make you happy.''

Her soul was bared. The distance mounted between them like a chasm. She stood to leave. ''Please, at least consider it.'' Her hands began shaking and she linked her fingers together. ''It's what I've really wanted to do with my life. Even Mother knew that.''

At the mention of her mother, Jonathan paled. Amanda wished there wasn't a need to broach the subject, but maybe the truth would convince him.

Jonathan rose to his feet. ''Amanda, I'm fully aware that you're an adult. I'm certain your professor thought this was a competent idea, but I can't approve of using your mother's endowment for this whimsical notion.''

Amanda felt the constriction in her throat as he admonished her. Her ideas were refuted and her hope vanished. She turned on her heel, heading for the stairs, and neared the top when the upstairs telephone's ring broke the silence. Wondering if Brandon had tried calling her at home, she lingered on the staircase, listening as her father answered.

"Chamberses' residence . . . Mick Terrence? Wait, let me take it in the study." Jonathan pressed the hold button and walked off toward his den. Hearing the name, Amanda's adrenaline rushed. She went to the upstairs phone and, never having eavesdropped before, carefully lifted the receiver. . . .

"Jonathan?" The British accent flowed. "Mick. Your old coworker."

"Yes. What causes you to ring?"

"There've been some problems afloat, Jonathan. Some real renewed interest in the case we faced a while ago. Articles are filling the *Daily* with talk of new evidence and a retrial."

"Retrial? That case had insufficient evidence. Why the switch?"

"Someone's been talking to the press, telling them the whole ordeal was a scam, Jon. I've already been subpoenaed. Word is out that you moved to avoid being summoned for a retrial. Our names are slandered in every newscast. Thought you might be interested in attending. It'd help your image in the papers, anyway."

"How serious is this trial?" Jonathan continued.

"Probably not bad. This 'evidence' can't be more than a pack of rumors. It's only in the magistrate's court. Shouldn't go before a jury."

"I'll arrange for the next flight possible."

"I'd appreciate that, Jon. Oh, you should also know

the publishing house is closed. That bloody new owner
is making it hard on everyone. My holiday pay is nearly
gone. The house isn't what it used to be, Jon.''

''I appreciate your ringing me. Be there soon.''

''Thought you'd want to know what's happening, Jon.
See you.''

Amanda replaced the receiver and went to her bedroom, locking the door.

As she changed clothes, a soft knock rapped on her
door. ''Coming,'' she answered, and peeked through a
small opening. ''Yes, Sara?''

Sara's eyes were large as coins. ''Amanda? Your
father is leaving soon on a flight to London. He's requested to see you. Right away!''

''London? Whatever for?'' She forced curiosity in her
voice, feeling the muscles tense in her neck.

''Don't rightly know,'' Sara whispered anxiously.
''He received a call, just now, and he's packing his suitcase.''

Amanda did know. Having overheard that the caller
was Mick Terrence was her sole motivation for eaves-
dropping. ''I'll be right down.'' She closed the door and
dressed in gray stirrup pants with a gray-and-pink striped
cotton shirt. She pushed the fitted sleeves to her elbows
as if ready to do battle, then left the serenity of her room.

Approaching her father's bedroom, Amanda watched
as he laid things onto the bed and searched through the
chest of drawers. She leaned against the doorjamb. ''Sara
told me you're leaving for London. Is someone in
need?''

''Yes, precisely.'' Her father's downcast eyes avoided

her in the same way he avoided explaining the whole situation.

She worried at why he would involve himself with Mick Terrence. Their move to America had calmed her fears over the rumors about Terrence. Now those fears were stirred. She wondered if her father knew of the stories of this man's illegalities. But Jonathan had never been one to tangle with criminal affairs. Amanda knew he could easily clear his name and come home. Nevertheless, she feared for him knowing the trip involved Terrence.

"How soon is your flight?"

"Ten-forty. Standby. They're certain I'll get on if I check in soon."

Amanda could smell the leather suitcase and it awakened memories of their move to the U.S., only a couple of months ago.

"I'll need you to call Benjamin tomorrow. Explain to him that I had to take emergency leave, will you? I'll be gone about two weeks."

"I'll tell him."

"And inform him that I want you to be consulted on any major decisions or extreme matters. I'm leaving the safe combinations and my set of keys with you. He and Mary can handle the actual business hours since he has a second set of keys, but I would prefer having you run the bank errands."

Amanda stared, surprised by his sudden confidence in her after the showdown in the living room. "Yes, certainly. I'll take care of them."

He snapped the suitcase together and grabbed his hat. "I'm also counting on you to hostess the publisher's cocktail party tomorrow. You've attended numerous occasions before. I'm sure you will do fine in my absence. Please extend my apologies." His tone was firm and he swept past her.

"Oh, and Amanda . . ." Jonathan stopped, half turned and stared down. "I owe you an apology. I shouldn't have raised my voice with you. However, I'm certain, given time, that you'll appreciate my position on the stable matter."

She swallowed, feeling the tension between them. How could he entrust her with his business and an important business reception without a second thought, and yet have so little confidence in her pursuing her own business?

After seeing her father to the door, Amanda returned to the solace of her room. Her mind swirled from the events of the last hour. She sat beside her camelback chest and pulled it open, studying her precious personal possessions. Lifting a thick spiral-bound volume, she glanced at the cover title: *The No-Horse-Sense Guide to Opening a Stable Business.* Smiling at the ludicrous title, she flipped the cover open to see the boldly scrawled *Excellent!* on the top page. She scanned the designs she'd meticulously researched for a year, checking out everything from veterinarians, to lighting, to kinds of feed.

Closing the book, Amanda peered down in the chest. An oblong, white box lay at the base. Lifting the small satin case, she opened it, beholding the lustrous strand of her mother's pearls—Amanda's sixteenth birthday present. They were the last gift she'd received from her mother. Amanda never wore them. She only cherished them. Viewing the miniature card that came with them, she read her mother's beautifully penned words, hearing the sound of her voice clear in her memory . . . *Never lose hope for your dreams. Love, Mother.*

Amanda sighed. She replaced the necklace in the case and clamped the lid shut. She knew how badly it would upset her father if she went on with her plans, but she had to. She had to follow her heart.

Chapter Six

Amanda checked her watch, then the phone. After seven hours of drawing stable plans in her father's office, the curiosity lingered. Had he called?

She tapped her pencil eraser on the desktop, staring out the window at the diminishing sunshine, contemplating whether to call home.

She had canceled her lessons. This morning's conversation with the club receptionist hung in her thoughts. She'd quickly expressed her rehearsed speech, explaining her father's absence. Then she'd darted out of the house, not allowing Brandon a chance to catch her. Staking the distance between them was crucial, but she hadn't expected to feel so sullen afterward.

She stared at the phone. "Oh, why not?" she said, and reached for it.

"Chamberses' residence," Sara's voice trilled through the receiver.

"Hello, Sara."

"Good afternoon, Amanda. How is everything at your father's shop?"

"Super. As I expected, Benjamin and Mary don't need me to lift a finger. In fact, I'm in the way, so I've spent the day reading in Daddy's office." Amanda paused. "Sara . . . did anyone ring for me?"

"Yes. About an hour ago."

Amanda's heartbeat quickened. "Who was it?"

"A lady by the name of Ms. Hargreaves. She asked me to inform you she would be late for the reception tonight."

"Ms. Hargreaves? The owner of Hargreaves' Stables?"

"Yes, I'm certain that's what she said."

"Peculiar," Amanda half mumbled to herself. "She's not in publishing. Did she mention who she'd be accompanying?"

"No. Is something the matter?"

"I suppose not. Actually I'm glad to hear she's attending. Thank you, Sara. I'll be home soon." She hung up the receiver and leaned back in her father's squeaky office chair. As frustrated as she'd been with Brandon last night, she was disappointed to find that he hadn't called. But hearing Ms. Hargreaves was attending the party overshadowed her feelings for him.

"Perfect. I'll offer to buy Brittany before the auction." She finished sketching her layout as Benjamin came upstairs and handed her a zippered bag for the bank.

"Thank you, Benjamin. See you tonight." She hurried out to the car.

On the way home, she rehearsed last-minute details for the reception, checking off a mental list. She'd instructed Barclay to handle deliveries and hire a valet attendant. Sara had finished the hors d'oeuvres this morning. At lunch Amanda had purchased a dress for entertaining. Everything was ready. Her enthusiasm started bubbling. Tonight was important.

Amanda strode through the garage door entrance to the house. With the dress slung over her arm, she hurried upstairs, calling for Sara. She freshened her makeup. She dabbed on several light touches of her favorite plumeria perfume. Then she changed into the dress. Its royal-blue satin swished as she put it on. She zipped it up, smoothed out the waves of hemline, and fluffed the short, pillowed sleeves. She turned to check the reverse side in the mirror, reassured that the scooped, open back was the sophisticated touch she needed for tonight's guests. "Oh, where are you, Sara?" she muttered excited to show off her good find.

She sat at her dressing table and brushed her hair, sweeping it up one side to fasten with a pearl-ornamented hair comb. Then she opened her camelback chest and lifted out the white satin case. As she lay the pearl strand around her neck memories of her mother worked into Amanda's heart, and a tear escaped, rolling down her cheek.

"I heard you, Amanda, but—" Sara bustled through the doorway and stopped, wide-eyed." Where did you find that dress? And . . . your pearls? Why, you've never worn them before."

"Aren't they lovely? I wanted to wait for a special occasion, and I thought Mother would have liked this."

Sara picked up her apron and dabbed at her eyes. "If only she could see you. You've become such a beautiful woman. And you're the exact image of her." Sara's voice began to break. She continued drying her tears and Amanda grabbed tissues for the both of them.

Sara sniffled. "I'd better go back to the hors d'oeuvres. Your guests will be arriving any moment."

Amanda checked her mascara and smoothed out the tear-streaked blush on her cheeks as two car doors shut. She shivered. Someone was here already. Being the hostess for her father's reception was no small affair. Sure, there would be other functions, but this was the paramount event—their first in America—the one that would leave a lasting impression. If she hosted the gala well, it'd be a feather in her cap. And she needed everything possible to convince her father to accept her independence.

Amanda pulled a blue box from the top shelf in her closet. She removed her white satin shoes, then slipped them on. She stood in front of the mirror once more. Pleased, a smile formed on her lips. Brandon's face suddenly crossed her mind. Though it was odd to think of him now, she envisioned seeing him tonight, dressed to the hilt. Her cheeks flushed. The mere thought of him in a tuxedo made her knees weak. Amanda was grateful he wouldn't be among the publishers tonight. The last thing she needed right now was to be distracted by his charming manner.

Door chimes dispelled her imaginary encounter. She hustled downstairs.

Sara, now wearing a lavender chiffon dress, served glasses of punch. The sweet aroma filled the room. Amanda passed the banquet table, laden with meats, cheeses, and hors d'oeuvres. Her stomach rumbled, but she was too nervous for even a bite. Barclay stood at the door in his gray tuxedo, helping two couples with their summer jackets.

Amanda welcomed each guest as they shuffled in, graciously listening to their thanks and compliments. She wondered if it was her imagination, or were people treating her with more respect in her father's absence?

An hour later, the ballroom was so crowded that Amanda hoped no more guests would arrive. Except Ms. Hargreaves. Though expected late, she had yet to make an appearance. The doorbell chimed once more, and Amanda turned her thoughts back to hosting.

"Miss Chambers." Barclay faced her. "Please welcome Ms. Olivia Hargreaves and Mr. Brandon Cordell." Barclay moved aside to stow the couple's belongings, obviously unaware of whom he'd just let in.

Every muscle in Amanda's body tensed and a flash of heat blazed within her. *How dare he invade my home, uninvited and undetected!* she thought angrily. She managed a perfect, though plastic, smile and willed control over her frozen tongue.

"Good evening, Ms. Hargreaves, Mr. Cordell." She nodded briefly in Brandon's direction, and returned her gaze to the older, sunlight-blond woman. "Thank you for coming. I apologize for my father's absence. He had to take an emergency trip to London. Please help yourself to hors d'oeuvres."

Ms. Hargreaves returned a smile, and tilted her trian-

gular face up to look fondly at Brandon. Her wedge hair-
cut dangled from the gesture. "Excuse me, Brandon,
dear, I'm going to snatch a glass of the punch."

Surprised by the short, thin woman's throaty voice,
Amanda watched as Olivia Hargreaves strolled toward
the tables. She guessed Olivia to be in her early thirties
and as flirtatious as Brandon. Yet, she wondered if the
bony woman was an intimate companion of his, or just
a friend.

Barclay stepped away and Amanda turned a fiery gaze
upon Brandon. The flame of indignation crept into her
face. She tried to show her disapproval, but her hard
stare did nothing to unnerve him. "How dare you invade
my home," she forced a normal tone of voice. "There
isn't a chance you received an invitation. My father and
I sent them all personally." She tried to keep her com-
posure, but the sight of him—dangerously attractive in
his black silk tux and emerald-green bow tie—wreaked
havoc on her self-control.

His gaze swept over her, taking in her elegant dress.
He smiled. Then he stepped close to her. "Why, Ms.
Chambers." His lowered voice drew her attention to his
mouth. "I should be offended by your outrageous manner as a hostess. But, since I am a gentleman . . . "

He reached for her hand and placed an invitation in
her palm. It was addressed to *Mr. Brandon Cordell and
Guest,* and, true enough, signed by Jonathan and herself.
Amanda blinked. Undeniably, she hadn't known him
then, and her father hadn't known him as Brandon. She
muffled a groan.

He studied her appearance, inattentive to her signs of
displeasure.

"Is that plumeria I smell? You are the vision of a flower, but you smell as lovely as one too," he teased in a playful, seductive voice.

"Clever of you to show, knowing my father wouldn't be here. Even Barclay didn't recognize you." She forced her smile so much she felt she was baring her teeth to bite him. The whole scene was unthinkable! Amanda could hardly believe the one person she'd really desired to visit with had arrived with the one person she really did *not* wish to see.

"Excuse me, Mr. Cordell, I have guests that I wish to entertain."

"I envy them," he countered, tilting an eyebrow.

His response distracted her and she paused, observing him again. He was entirely too appealing, dressed as formally as a bridegroom. Forgetting her lingering gaze, a part of her wished for a groom like Brandon. Confident, intelligent, attractive, daring . . .

"Is there something else?" His voice recaptured her thoughts. "You have a look of desire in those gorgeous blue eyes."

Chagrined, she tried to keep herself from blushing. How did he do it? He'd seen right through her pretense. He knew she was melting like butter. She wished he didn't have such intuition about her feelings. "Excuse me." Amanda whirled and migrated to another group of people.

For nearly an hour, she conversed with the guests, always keeping her eye on Olivia, but to no avail. The woman was always on Brandon's sleeve. Amanda half listened to a publisher from Richmond relay his irritation with being audited, when finally she noticed Olivia alone. She politely excused herself and threaded her way across the crowded room, observing the skinny woman again. Nice smile, Amanda thought, but her deep voice, long straight nose, and bony cheeks granted her a snobbish air.

Nonetheless, Olivia was selling her horses, and Amanda wanted to buy. If the party was making a favorable impression, she could possibly wing a private deal on Brittany. Amanda took a deep breath. She lifted a glass of punch from the table and steeled herself for her business proposal.

"Ms. Hargreaves?" she called. "Olivia, isn't it?"

"Yes. Oh, lovely gathering, dear."

"I'm pleased you're here." Amanda smiled, repelled only by her escort.

"Thank you. It's a shame your father's away. I wanted to meet him."

"There'll be another opportunity. I'd like to divulge a little secret of mine, if I may."

"Certainly. I love a good piece of gossip!" Olivia gave a breathy laugh and sipped her drink.

"I'm a new member at your stables. I've heard you're selling the horses. I'm quite interested in some, for starting my own business. Is it true you'll be selling them all at the end of summer?"

"Yes." The woman seized another glass as Sara passed by. "Which horses are you interested in?"

"One in particular. Brittany—the black Arabian mare. I'm certain I could match a fair price."

"I appreciate your offer, dear, but taking the horses to auction is part of the contract I'm under. You understand." She took a long drink of the punch. "Sorry I couldn't bend the rules a bit, but I'm obligated."

"Of course." Amanda grinned politely, but she was disheartened by the reappearing competition. Perhaps the auction prices wouldn't range terribly high, she thought. Nonetheless, it was unwise to commit to anything more than temporary plans, since she still had to convince her father. "Pardon me for asking, but how much is an average price at auction?"

"Well, these are quality-bred horses, most retired from racing and top show backgrounds. At least ten thousand dollars. The auction will likely start them at eight to promote bids. A fine horse like Brittany could reach fifteen, hopefully more." She gave a spirited laugh and sipped her drink.

"Fifteen thousand?" Amanda winced, but tried to hide it. Her business would need at least that to get started. She fingered the strand of pearls, calculating English pounds into dollars. Then she took a large swallow of her punch, ignoring the tart fruitiness biting her taste buds.

"Sounds like a lot of money." Brandon's deep voice entered the conversation. "But I'm *sure* your father is in full support of the idea." He pricked her assurance, squinting his eyes knowingly at Amanda.

"Mr. Cordell." Amanda gave a curt smile. "I wasn't aware you were listening in."

"If you'd like suggestions from someone experienced, I have a few."

"I don't think that will be necessary." She felt her confidence rising, along with a temptation to be sarcastic. "I have a minor in business, and I'm an accomplished ballerina. If I can't work through a problem, I'll just tiptoe.''

Olivia let out a laugh, turning heads around them. Then she grabbed for a new glass of punch and draped her hand on Amanda's shoulder. ''Really, dear, you should take his advice. When it comes to maneuvering, Brandon certainly knows what's best.'' The woman gave him a dramatic wink.

Flustered, Amanda sipped her drink, wondering what maneuvers Olivia was referring to. Nevertheless, she decided to oblige him, not wanting to make a scene. ''Well, Brandon, what should I look into first?''

''Simple.'' his blue eyes grew intent. ''If you need financing, avoid getting a loan. You can save interest and fees by finding a partner or two. Someone willing to take a risk and make a profitable return.''

Amanda beamed theatrically. ''I see you attended the same business classes. Didn't you have some unique advice?''

''Not unique—experienced. I know *when* to make the right moves.'' Brandon steeled his gaze back at her, making her nervous. He set down his glass and placed his hand against the bared part of Amanda's back. ''Excuse us, Olivia,'' he announced, clutching Amanda's elbow with his other hand and compelling her to walk outside, onto the terrace.

Her senses awakened where his hands touched her skin. Tingly bumps raised upon her arms. Once on the porch and out of earshot, she pulled from his grasp. ''You are intolerable!'' she chided. ''How could you come here, knowing full well that my father despises you, and then embarrass me when I'm conducting business matters? Which are *none* of your concern!''

''You would do well to learn from me, Amanda.'' Gone was his playful tone. His inflection now had a serious, almost desperate, edge. ''I could teach you tricks most professionals don't even know exist.''

She lifted her chin with determination, but it was no use. Her willpower was dissolving quickly. She was no match for his seductive way. She turned to stand at the trestle, staring at the fading sunset. Honeysuckle and tea roses permeated the air with their confectionery smells, and the tranquil outdoors began evaporating her turbulent emotions. She wondered if he really had some words of wisdom, some insight to help her attain her dream. Maybe she should listen. After all, he did run a publishing house.

''Bran—'' She turned and bumped against him, as he'd moved directly behind her.

''I'm sorry you canceled your lessons.''

She searched his handsome face, glowing from the sunset's rays. His passionate expression revealed the longing she knew existed. Again, the strange twinges of familiarity rose inside her. She retraced her memory, trying to understand why she always *almost* recognized him.

''I'm the real reason. Right? Not your father's leave of absence.''

''How perceptive,'' she remarked, struggling to remember his scandals.

''If you quit because of me—'' His voice took on a strange, reserved tone. ''—then you've made up your mind about where your loyalties lie.''

"Loyalties?"

"Whether you trust me, or your father."

"And I should trust you? Don't make me laugh. You've never offered me one explanation. Why should I shower you with loyalty?" She'd really wanted to tell him how she'd ached to see him again, but the confession was entirely too dangerous when he stood so close to her.

"Amanda . . . " The last streak of sunlight reflected in his eyes. He lifted her hand and softly kissed her palm. "Please. Trust me."

His switch to sensitivity made her breathing irregular and she drew back her hand. "How can I do that, Brandon? I don't even know why you're living under an assumed name. Explain that to me." Hearing her own quavering voice, she backed against the terrace wall to avoid him physically. But Brandon stepped nearer, pinning her next to the warm brick, his face inches from hers.

Why can't he tell me? she wondered skeptically, resentful of his silence. "Your eyes have answers, Brandon, but your lips say nothing." She paused, giving him one last chance. "I can't trust you."

She pushed beside him and started for the terrace doorway, but he latched on to her wrist. She twisted, but his grasp held and he brought his other hand up behind her head.

"I can't explain what you want to hear," he whispered forcefully, bearing down his gaze, pulling her closer, narrowing the gap between their lips." And I won't force you to trust me. But I want to hear you say it from your heart, not your head. Tell me you don't feel the passion burning right now. Tell me that you never ache when I touch you and look into your eyes. If you can swear that my kiss does nothing to you . . . *then* I'll believe you can't trust me.''

His breath floated against her cheek and her head pounded with the rush of fury and longing. She knew it would be a lie to claim indifference, and she struggled not to collapse in his embrace. To admit her attraction to him would fan the fire, and provoke her father's anger. And if *that* happened, she would destroy her remaining chances to start her business. Amanda looked away, not able to face him.

''It meant nothing to me.'' She uttered the only words that could end this madness, regretting the need for them.

''You're lying. Look in my eyes and tell me again.''

Amanda wished she could disappear. He had seen right through her. Bravely, she met his powerful gaze. ''It meant nothing to—''

He pulled her against him in the fading light, silencing her lips with his kiss, clutching her tightly with one arm and trailing his hand down her back with the other. Amanda tried pushing him away, but her attempts were futile against his strength. She finally stopped struggling and his kiss softened, luring her willingness to be loved. His fingers caressed between her shoulder blades.

''Tell me again,'' he whispered in her ear. ''I want to hear you say it when I'm touching you.''

It's so unfair! Amanda churned, as fervor rose inside her. His lips had melted all her defenses. Why did she dissolve so easily? Where was her fortitude? She finally looked into his dusk-darkened face, feeling the urge to bare her heart . . . to trust him.

A shattering crash came from the ballroom. Amanda wrenched her head up, her eyes wide. She fled from Brandon's warmth, hurrying inside to inspect the damage. The alarmed crowd was silent. Sara stood behind the table looking down at the floor, pale-faced in horror.

"Sara! What is it?" Amanda hadn't intended to shriek and she cleared her throat, remembering her guests.

But Sara stood, spellbound, and Amanda was forced to see for herself. She edged her way around the table's end and gasped at the petrifying scene. The white table linen was splattered red and pieces of green glass were everywhere. There on the floor, motionless, lay Olivia Hargreaves.

Chapter Seven

Amanda stood over her guest. "Barclay! Call 911. Sara! Fetch some towels."

"Amanda, I'm sorry!" Sara quavered. "I didn't see her fall."

"Sara—towels. Now!" Amanda ordered.

Brandon stood at Olivia's side and kicked large pieces of glass away from where she lay. Bending, he checked for a pulse. He gave Amanda an assuring nod. "She's breathing. But she's out cold."

Upon a closer look, Amanda now realized that the red stains were not, in fact, her guest's lifeblood, but the punch which had splattered upon impact. Olivia had brought a number of filled glasses down with her.

"This is a disaster," she whispered, and held her fists against her stomach, shaking from nerves. *Stay calm. You've been through a worse accident yourself, and all alone at that,* she coaxed herself as minutes passed. But the high-pitched sirens of the nearing ambulance compounded her panic, and she rushed outside to get away from the dreadful sight.

"You all right?" Brandon asked, having followed her. He placed a strong hand on her shoulders and lifted her chin.

"Yes, I'm sorry. I shouldn't be acting so childishly."

"There's no need to apologize for your reaction."

She looked into his face, seeing real concern. "Thank you."

In the darkening eve they watched the emergency vehicle pull up the drive, bright lights whirling. Paramedics followed Brandon into the house with a stretcher and Amanda walked in behind them, trying to fight the shock and nausea. They checked Olivia's vital signs and asked if anyone knew if she'd been ill. Then they cleaned the glass off of her, checked for serious cuts, and lifted her onto the stretcher. Quickly, they wheeled her to the ambulance and raised her inside.

"I must come along," Amanda begged the attendant. "I'm the hostess. I'm responsible." Preparing to hop into the ambulance, she felt someone grab her forearm. Brandon faced her squarely.

"I think it'd be best if you stayed. Your quests are disturbed and they need to be put at ease. I'll take care of everything here."

Somehow, she knew he could handle whatever he claimed to, though she didn't know why or how she understood that.

"I'm the hostess," she protested, feeling her stomach

twist as she imagined telling her father. ''They'll need papers signed. I have to.''

''Amanda, trust me,'' he persisted. ''I'll see that everything is taken care of. Now, go. Relieve your guests and assure them Olivia will be fine.''

His direct, sensible voice soothed away her apprehension. She nodded. Then he leaped into the ambulance, and the paramedic swung the door shut. In seconds the vehicle disappeared beyond the hedged driveway. Amanda stood, suspended in awe over the way Brandon had calmed and encouraged her.

She returned to the ballroom. Sara had cleaned up the mess. Despite the alarmed looks on faces, Amanda reported that Olivia's condition was improved, and her fall was due to a low blood pressure condition. Amanda smiled, but easing the crowd was futile. They excused themselves one by one, expressing awkward good-byes. Benjamin and Mary were last to leave and Amanda clutched Benjamin's arm.

''Not a word of this to my father. I'll explain when he returns.''

They nodded simultaneously, and left.

Amanda was convinced—the evening was going to hold grave impact. Not only that, Olivia's accident released a black cloud of insecurity in Amanda. She now doubted her ability to handle stressful situations. Her own accident resurfaced and the memory loomed, along with fears of being responsible for someone else's injuries if she started her own business.

She headed for her room, wishing the whole tragedy would disappear. But as she walked upstairs, the trepidation made her stomach turn. She sprinted the remaining stairs and ran into the bathroom. She reached for the faucet and turned it on with trembling hands. She cupped the cool liquid to wet her face. It helped. She began to feel stable again. As she reached for a glass she caught her washed-out appearance in the mirror and grimaced at the reflection of her fright.

"Trust me." Brandon's assurance echoed inside her. No matter what the circumstance, his plea remained the same. Every time their paths crossed, he struggled to gain her faith, her willingness to lean on him. But assurance wasn't the only feeling she had around him. And being romantically drawn to him at the risk of losing her dream wasn't part of her plan. *Even if she could trust him, she couldn't let him interfere.*

After a pathetic night of insomnia, Amanda rose at seven-thirty. Quickly dressing into some shorts and a cotton blouse, she drove to Hargreaves' Stables. She had to know how Olivia was doing.

She enjoyed the morning drive in the cascading sunshine. The peaceful Virginia morning helped drown out the fears of last night. She pulled into the parking lot, just as Finley was opening the office.

"'Morning!'' He gave her a surprised look, and opened the door for them.

"Good morning. I don't suppose you've heard from Ms. Hargreaves?"

"Yeah, I have at that." He smiled, seemingly not too concerned about the accident. "She called this morning, told me she just woke up in the hospital, wonderin' what happened. I'm glad Mr. Cordell already called me."

"Is she feeling better?"

"Well, she's got a sprained shoulder and some cuts, but aside from that I heard she was doin' fine. Be back in the swing in a couple of weeks."

"Was she . . . upset, about the party?" Amanda ventured, hoping he'd received indication of whether the woman was going to file a suit against her.

"Oh, no. She said she was havin' a wonderful time, until she slipped. But I wouldn't expect her to take it out on you."

Evidently Olivia hadn't wanted her employee to know *why* she slipped, so Amanda kept quiet about her condition. "Good. I'll call the hospital tomorrow and talk to her. Would you fetch me some tack? I think I'll ride Brittany this morning."

"Sure. But where are your fancy ridin' clothes?" He glanced down at her rolled-up denim shorts and pink cotton shirt, and smiled.

"I decided to give regular ones a try," she said.

He nodded. "You're attached to Brittany, aren't you?"

"She's wonderful. It's too bad about the auction in fall. I would have tried to purchase her directly from Olivia, but she told me she was obligated to take them all to auction."

"Ms. Hargreaves said that, now did she?" His narrowing, red eyebrows crinkled his forehead with deep grooves.

"Yes. Last night. She said it was part of a contract she'd signed, to auction all the horses without direct buying. Didn't you know?"

"No. And since I was with her when she signed the

contract, I'd say it's a little suspicious. There's no clause in the contract referring to the horses at all. That was strictly Ms. Hargreaves' decision. But aside from all of that, Brittany's not even on the list.''

"But you'd said she was going in the fall.''

"I thought she was. But I reviewed the list this morning and Brittany's name was removed—erased.''

"You don't think she's already sold Brittany?'' Amanda's hope plummeted.

"There's one way to find out. Look in the books. I can check up to last Monday. If it happened before then, it'd be in the last log, and all the back logs are kept in her home safe.''

"Well, I suppose there isn't much else to do but talk to her. But if you hear of something, Mr. Finley, would you let me know?''

"You bet,'' he answered, heading for the tack room.

"Thank you.'' She took the tack and left for the stalls.

Reaching Brittany, Amanda gave the mare a loving pat, and smoothed her hand down the animal's neck. "How's my lady today?'' Amanda cooed affectionately, then she gave Brittany an apple she'd brought from home. The horse crunched and slobbered, devouring it in no time. Then, flaring her nostrils and stomping her hoofs, she trotted circles in her stall.

"Ready for sunshine and green pastures?'' Amanda said. Brittany whinnied in response, pricking up her ears and tossing her head.

After her ride, Amanda drove home and rounded the last corner of the driveway. She emerged from the tall hedges. "No!'' She hit the brakes, reflexing at first sight of the black Alfa Romeo parked by the fountain.

He's here, she said to herself, feeling the thump-thump of her heart. Amanda had regained a little will-power after the close encounter with Brandon on the terrace. She didn't want to lose it. She pulled the car into the opened garage and cut the motor. The engine clicked in the silence. She debated staying in the car, but she wanted to know how Olivia was doing. Tucking her purse under her arm, she went in through the kitchen. Brandon's deep voice made her shiver and she was tempted to dash upstairs without being seen. Then she heard Brandon say "I'll check back," and she knew she had to face him sooner or later. She walked on in.

"Heavens!" Barclay sputtered. "Seems she's here after all."

"Yes, I see." Brandon nodded, lifting an eyebrow.

"Mr. Cordell wishes to see you," Barclay announced. But Amanda could tell that Brandon was already seeing her, as he surveyed her bared legs. His examining eyes made her uncomfortable. A memory flashed of their embrace on the terrace, and her breathing constricted. "Thank you, Barclay. I'll see Mr. Cordell in the study, after I change clothes."

"I don't have much time," Brandon spoke sternly. "I have a lesson in half an hour. I'll be brief."

She nodded her approval to Barclay, and then led Brandon to her father's den. Once inside, he closed the wooden door. It fastened with a snap.

"First things first," he said, then paused pensively.

Amanda waited. He perched on the arm of the sofa; the muscles in his legs were taut, ready to spring. Evidence of his fitness. Or uneasiness? Her pulse quickened. She forced her attention up to his dark blue eyes.

"Olivia's going to be fine after last night's mishap."

She breathed easier, relieved he hadn't come to discuss private matters. "Yes, I've been to the stables. Which reminds me, do you know anything about Brittany not going to auction this fall?"

Brandon stood to look at Jonathan's bookcase. "No."

"Last night, Olivia specifically told me *all* the horses were going to auction as part of her contract. This morning I find out from Mr. Finley that Brittany's name was removed from the list."

"Maybe just an oversight. In any case"—he returned to his own topic—"Olivia now has a sprained shoulder to nurse for a couple of weeks. And I came to ask you something." He paused, looking optimistic.

"Yes?"

"Her stables are going to suffer unless she can get some temporary help. Finley's already doing the early shift and the weekends. Between the two of them Olivia hasn't ever hired anyone else. I've offered to help out on weeknights since I don't instruct after three o'clock."

Amanda wondered what this had to do with her. Finally, he faced her.

"I suggested to Olivia that she let you help me run the stables."

Amanda pictured herself in the stable office, busily running things.

"She already knows about your interest in the horses and a business of your own . . . and she likes you."

"Likes me?" Her brows scrunched. "After last night?"

"Yeah. Would you be up to it?" he asked in a businesslike manner.

Her delight was interrupted by the reality of working next to Brandon for two weeks. If she agreed, she'd be getting good training. On the other hand . . . she remembered his kiss last night and the wave of adrenaline spurred her to answer. "I appreciate what you did, but—" She shook her head as a replacement for words. His serious expression showed he wanted an explanation. "I have rehearsals, thirty hours a week. If I don't ace every one I'll be disqualified from auditions. I'm ready to drop when I come home."

"What'll happen to your auditions when you open up your own business? You can't do both."

Amanda already knew the irony of her situation. But she had no choice. Without her father's support, she needed to stay in the company. At least until her plans were complete enough to go on without his approval.

"I can't. I'm already spending my spare time at the publishing house. I just couldn't juggle all three," she defended her answer, but the words seemed meaningless. She wanted to say yes.

Brandon stared frankly, as though he read her mind. He obviously didn't believe a word. "Your father's business closes at five. You could help me five times a week. Then it won't take all your spare time."

What if Daddy finds out? Guilt nagged her, though she had yet to commit to the plan. She weighed the pros and cons. She desperately wanted the experience, but she'd been trying to minimize her problems by staying away from Brandon. It was the only way to improve her chances with her father. Painfully, she had to deny his offer. "Sorry."

Brandon only blinked. He didn't seem affected by her decision.

"Well, I won't argue this one with you, Amanda. I thought you'd want some hands-on experience. But it's your choice." He started for the door.

Seeing him leave so quickly cut her like a razor. "Wait!" she blurted, suddenly unsure of her answer. She searched his questioning eyes. A flicker of hope seemed to dance in them, a sparkle that assured her to follow her instincts. "Very well. But only four times a week. No more," she stated.

"All right." He nodded.

She barely breathed, anxious over his presence. He stood at the door, looking her over eagerly. She sensed there was more beneath the surface conversation, and she tried to understand more through his eyes.

"There's something else we need to discuss." He stepped beside her and slowly reached for her face.

Amanda felt limp. She hungered for his kiss, but he only held her chin.

"You can be sure I'll keep our relationship at the stables strictly professional. You need to admit some things to yourself. Until you can, I'm not going to persuade you any further. But I've waited a long time for you, Amanda." He paused, glancing at her lips. "I can only wait a while longer."

Waited a long time? She just met him a couple of weeks ago. And yet his words stirred those familiar feelings again. Still the images in her mind were hazy, unclear. He leaned slightly forward, but stopped short of contact, then retreated, leaving the den. Her adrenaline raced.

Through the window, she saw him hop in his car. He drove away. Amanda felt limp and numb. She ached for his touch.

The sudden ring of the telephone jarred her from her fixation. "Chambers," her listless answer tumbled off her lips.

"Amanda? It's Father. Are you all right? You don't sound well."

"Daddy?" She bounced back to reality. "No, I'm fine. Just a bit tired, after the party last night."

"Yes, how was the reception?"

"Oh . . . it'll be an evening not soon forgotten."

"Excellent. I called to confirm that I should be home in a couple of weeks, as expected. How's Benjamin? Has he needed much help?"

Amanda noticed he'd quickly changed the subject, and she wondered how the trial was going. "No. He's holding up nicely, doing a fine job. I hardly need to be around, except for the bank runs, which I rather think he could handle also."

"Tell him I want a good report when I return. And don't worry about the printing deadlines, dear. He'll know what to do."

"Yes, Daddy."

"'Bye, darling. Please tell Sara and Barclay I telephoned, will you?"

"Yes. Good-bye."

She hung up the receiver, feeling the clenching in her stomach. *Relax, you'll explain the rest at a more suitable time—after Olivia's recovery*, she told herself soothingly.

* * *

The July nights were bathed in heat. Brandon's actions confirmed his promise of professional behavior. Amanda was even beginning to relax around him, absorbed in his exceptional knowledge about running a business. She took in all the tips she could assimilate for future reference. It was refreshing to work around him when he wasn't fueling her emotions and making her feel so vulnerable. There were occasions, however, when reaching for a pencil or stack of papers, they briefly touched and met each other's gaze, then went back to their work. Her skin tingled from their contact, and it took a while to regain her focus. But the instances were brief and Brandon continued to act normally, seemingly not aware of the same electrifying surges she'd felt.

The Fourth of July neared and Sara reluctantly agreed to watch the fireworks display with Amanda, which were now just over a week away. Fortunately, Amanda's rehearsals seemed to blur past as the days went by and she buried herself in enthusiasm over her nightly responsibilities. She never gave ballet a second thought once she left the dance floor.

After the first week, she'd grown quite attached to the horses and comfortable with her charge over them. She set out one night to start the feeding rounds while Brandon closed up the till. She grabbed a bucket and dug into the oat barrel, then passed the stalls and dispensed a portion to each ravenous horse. As she poured feed into their bins, she felt a subtle assurance that she was doing the right thing. Now she needed to talk to her father again. In her heart, she wanted to pursue her idea with or without his blessing. But she was reluctant to sever possibilities of convincing him to support her. Giving it time could only help.

She went back for another bucketful and fed the other side of whinnying horses. As the animals eagerly crunched their dinner, she cut open a bale of hay and tore sections off, setting off down the aisle to distribute a square to each tenant. Then she made a final round with the hose, talking sweetly to each animal as she filled their water containers.

Amanda put the hose away, rolling it around the hanger. She checked on the tack room to make sure everything had been put away. After she switched off the light, she backed out of the tack room and shut the door. Turning, she was startled to see Brandon watching her from the entrance of the sliding stable doors.

"I came down to help, but it looks like you've finished."

She smiled at his offer. "You looked rather busy, so I thought I'd take care of it." She walked over to Brittany's quarters and leaned upon the stall door, watching the mare chomping her grain with zeal.

Brandon checked his watch. "You handled them yourself, in record time. You'll be ready to open up your own business in no time."

She nodded. "I've been ready to do that for years."

"Do you have concrete plans, other than the horses?"

She looked his way. His hair looked black in the dusk-lit barn. "I have a volume—filled with research and preparation—two inches thick. It's all my own work. Everything needed to open and operate a stable riding business." She noticed that he looked impressed. He came up to lean beside her, resting his chin upon his crossed arms. The smells of hay and straw mingled with the citrus scent of his aftershave. "Plus my new expertise, thanks to you." She offered a grateful smile.

Brandon tilted his head and looked at her thoughtfully. "I want you to have the best advantage possible. I'd really like to see you catch your dream, Amanda." Then he looked away. "Even if I can't be part of it."

Her line of vision dropped to the stall floor and blurred in the yellow straw. She felt a sting of tears rise behind her eyes. Why did he always want the best for her? How could he care so much? She reflected upon her father's suspicions, wondering if they were at all founded.

"Believe me, you've played a large part," she mumbled.

"Would you show me your plans sometime? I'd like to see what you've come up with."

She gave him a surprised, eager look. "Actually, they're in my car. I've been working on them at the publishing house."

"May I see them? Unless you need to get home."

"I have a few minutes," she agreed, and trotted to her car to retrieve the bound leaflet and roll of sketches she'd almost finished.

Inside, she spread her foundation sketches on the office table, pointing out the designs. "My aim is to start with six horses, but I'll need to have at least twelve stalls for growth. Most of them can be used for tack, feed, and straw in the meantime. The extra storage would help cut costs for building a storage barn, as well as having room to expand without further costs. Medicine supplies would be locked up, over here." She pointed the pencil to a corner stall on the prints.

"What're these?"

"Skylights. One pane over each pair of stalls for additional light."

"That's very good." He glanced her way, showing his approval.

His praise over her ideas made Amanda even more certain that she was on the right track. Now, if she could only convince Daddy. She released a sigh, rerolling the drafts. Brandon leafed through her volume on stable businesses, scanning parts of each chapter.

"It looks like you really did your homework on this one."

"I gathered the research over four years—for myself, not the class. But since our final was to prepare and demonstrate how to open up a business, I knew I'd already accumulated all the information I needed. My remaining task was to include a proposal and have the information organized and bound."

"You've been dreaming about this for a long time, hmm?"

The sincerity in his eyes tugged at Amanda's heart. She'd seen so little of Brandon's personal interest in the last twelve days. His distance from her—physically and emotionally—had gradually fanned her desire to be closer to him. Now she was drowning in the sensitive blue depths of his eyes. They revealed longing, a desire to remove the restraint that held him back.

"I should be on my way," she whispered, and reached for the leaflet.

"Good-night, Amanda. And thank you."

"For what?"

"For sharing your dreams with me."

Warmth blanketed her. She longed to hug him. But she couldn't. Since she'd started working with Brandon, she'd had an uncanny sense they were striving together for the same goal, almost like partners. Now she felt it with a certainty. If only her father cared for her dreams a fraction of the way Brandon did. She smiled gratefully and fought the tears that threatened to spill. ''Thanks for enjoying them.''

The following night Amanda tallied up the supply order for feed, vitamins, grooming brushes, and salt tablets. Pages flapped across the table from her. She glanced at Brandon who was inspecting the stables' account ledger from last month—the same ledger Sam Finley had said was locked up in Olivia's home safe. Intently, Brandon began punching numbers into an old adding machine. It responded to his rapid keying with a noisy *tick-tick-whirr-whirr*. After several curls of tape, he stopped to look at the final amount.

''Why last month?'' she asked.

''Hmm? Oh, I needed to verify some figures.''

''Like?''

''Oh, nothing. Just a glitch I wanted to check. It panned out.''

Glitch? she thought. What was he up to? Amanda perused her supply order, but tried, casually, to keep an eye on Brandon, to spot anything unusual.

Later, he stood, stretching. Then he went downstairs to make some coffee. Amanda quickly scanned the ledger, seeing if the glitch had anything to do with Brittany. She examined each day, finding nothing to indicate any horses had been sold. However, she did find a sus-

piciously large deposit—twenty-one thousand dollars—
with no documented reason. It didn't take a genius to
understand. The likelihood increased that Olivia had already sold Brittany. But if that was true, why had the
woman kept it a secret? What would've motivated her
to lie to Amanda? *I'll bet Brandon knows,* Amanda
thought, nursing her hunch.

Hearing his approaching footsteps on the wood-
planked stairs, she flipped the ledger back to its original
place and returned her attention to her paperwork. Brandon sat down with two steaming mugs of fresh coffee
and, after a brief smile, resumed tackling his numbers.
Her assumptions evaporated. Maybe he didn't know. He
hadn't given any indication of it.

Surprised by her suspicions, Amanda concluded it was
more likely that the large deposit was a partial payment
for the sale of the stables, and the auction list was simply
an error. She decided she was working too hard. Perhaps
fatigue and her desire to own Brittany were fabricating
strange notions in her head. Besides, Brandon had clearly
told her he didn't know anything about Brittany being
sold. Surely he'd have mentioned it to her.

Amanda helped Brandon balance the books late Friday
evening. It was their final night together. She watched
him, focused upon the task of calculating. *"You'd do
well to learn from me. I could teach you tricks most
professionals don't even know exist."* His earlier claim
replayed in her mind as she observed him penciling in
the log. The night of the reception, his words had merely
seemed proud. Now she saw the truth of them. Over the
last two weeks she'd learned to trust him, the way an

amateur learns from the master. Though she'd complied with their arrangement for other reasons, she now reflected upon his proven wisdom of running a business. Her time under his wing was invaluable. She'd found him intelligent and instinctive, never giving in to second best. *If he were in charge of my business I would trust him.* She silently affirmed her new opinion.

Brandon tossed his pencil onto the table. He leaned back in the wooden chair and it creaked. Stretching, he let out a roaring sigh of accomplishment, then laced his hands behind his head. Amanda watched the tension leave his muscular body as he relaxed.

"Well, Amanda, our mission is accomplished. I'm sure Olivia won't fall to pieces when we tell her we've expanded her bank account while she was laid up. She's coming back to more money than she's made in months."

"It hardly seems fair she should benefit from ruining my father's reception." Her playful sarcasm flowed, in spite of her relief that Olivia was okay, and their combined efforts had paid off so nicely.

Brandon leaned forward, smiling. His face was darkened by a tiny growth of whiskers. The earnestness in his eyes severed her ability to reason. In their alluring blue depths she sensed again the hazy impressions of déjà vu. But still she wasn't able to bring them into focus.

"Did I mention how stunning you were in that dress?"

His compliment broke into her drifting thoughts. "Hmm? Yes. You said something about a flower," she answered. They paused in silence, and Amanda felt the energy in the air between them.

"I hope this was a profitable experience, Amanda." He folded his arms. The navy cotton polo pulled taut against his chest.

Amanda remembered the solid warmth of his chest when he'd cornered her on the terrace patio. "It—yes, it was f-fine," she stammered, trying to transport her thoughts off of his body. "And very helpful. I do admit, you know quite a bit about enterprise strategies."

"That's amazing. We actually agree on something." She smiled.

"Thank you," Brandon said softly. "I know that was difficult. It's not easy to admit when you're mistaken about someone."

Amanda absorbed the words, discerning their double meaning. She had been wrong about him, and she wanted to admit that she felt differently now.

"Amanda . . . what would you say to joining me for a cool drink at the club? I need to go back to my office and pick up some things before I head off to the cabin this weekend."

She watched him. He turned the pencil end over end, like a shy teenager beseeching a date. For two weeks they'd worked side by side, and he'd never given any indication that he'd want to spend time with her . . . afterward.

"The lounge is open for a while," he continued. "We could celebrate our teamwork efforts."

Amanda's eyes felt dry as she stared long at him, looking for signs, reasons to say no. She couldn't think of any.

"Well?" he asked, placing the pencil down and folding his hands.

" 'Strictly professional' relationship, hmm?"

Brandon remained silent, but in his eyes she saw vulnerability and need.

There couldn't be harm in one drink with him. "Think we're dressed appropriately?" She glanced at her violet summer top and denim shorts.

"You look great." He barely whispered the words.

Chapter Eight

Amanda made a call to Sara, telling her not to wait up. Then she turned to Brandon who stood, keys in hand, by the door. "Ready," she announced.

"My car." He switched off the lights and locked up the office, then held the door open for her.

Reaching the club parking lot, they saw crowds of people milling around. "What's the hubbub?" she asked.

"It must be the Independence Dance. I hadn't expected it to attract so many. We can go elsewhere. I just need to stop in my office a second."

They walked in the lobby and Amanda listened to the saxophone player, blowing slow, rhythmic tones. She liked the relaxing mood in the tempo.

With the resonant music, Brandon spoke close to her ear. "Would you like to stay and listen while I get my

107

things?'' His lips brushed her earlobe. Tingling surged through Amanda's neck at the scant contact. She nodded. Then Brandon slipped away, down the hall.

She leaned against the lobby wall and listened. Modestly, she swayed to its rhythm. Several people passed through, mostly couples. Then a cluster of young guys walked past, obviously in search of a date. Some of them smiled at her, others made comments and stared, making her uncomfortable. They went to the other side of the hallway and stood in a huddle. What was taking him so long? With Brandon's absence, the gawking strangers made her insecure.

Then she realized one in the group of young men started pointing at her, teasing the youngest-looking one. After a minute of badgering from his buddies, he took the challenge to approach her. Amanda turned to look away.

Brandon, where are you? she thought in panic, expectantly watching the hall for signs of him. Finally she saw him returning. She smiled and waved eagerly, then edged her way through the closely knit people to meet him. She latched onto his arm and chanced a look back at the young guy. Fortunately, her gestures toward Brandon had stonewalled the kid's intentions, and she saw him rejoin his laughing friends.

Brandon's return couldn't have been timed better. Yet her amorous behavior wasn't solely to avoid the stranger. With the romantic music, she'd been lingering on the memories of Brandon's kisses. He put his arm around her shoulders, apparently not offended by her display of affection. They walked over to the dance hall's swarmed entrance.

Numerous candlelit tables dotted the darkness with flag-patterned circles. Each face in the crowd was softly illuminated by the candle glow, and most of the audience was smiling. The dance floor was also packed. Couples hugged tenderly as they danced to the slow number.

"He's really good, isn't he?" Brandon gently spoke near her ear.

She nodded and smiled. "Yes. Wonderful. I'd like to stay, but getting a table doesn't look too favorable."

"Where there's a will, there's a way." Brandon took her hand. They wound through people, between tables and finally up to a blond waitress. He whispered something in the woman's ear and she nodded, said something back, then led them up front, off to the side to an empty table marked RESERVED.

The waitress nabbed the sign and Brandon pulled the chair out for Amanda. The song ended, and in the lull after the applause, the waitress asked to take their orders.

"Soda?" Brandon's eyes twinkled in the stage lighting.

"Sure."

He turned to the waitress. "Two sodas." The woman scribbled and smiled. Then he handed her a twenty-dollar bill. She thanked him, then squeezed past to return to the bar.

Curious, Amanda stared at Brandon. The band started in again with a livelier song, adding some strong bass and electric piano to the saxophone. "How did you manage this?" she asked.

"I've known that waitress for years." He spoke directly at her, raising his voice a little above the music.

"The party that reserved this table is really late. And an empty table is not in her best interest."

He could probably talk any woman into doing anything, Amanda thought, and considered it wise to remember his charms.

"Your turn for confession." His inquisitive eyes fixed upon her.

"Confession?"

"Why'd you make a dash for me, like I was your long-lost love?"

"Oh," she said, feeling the bashful smile spread on her face. "I was a little nervous. There was a group of young fellows gaping at me. I was afraid of being asked for a dance. It's just that . . . I'm not very experienced, especially with the romantic way of dancing."

He watched her attentively. She tried to discern his thoughts, but came up dry. The waitress returned with frosty glasses, set them down, and left again. Still Amanda noticed Brandon's gaze on her. He had that hungry look again. She sipped her limy drink, feeling flush over his stare.

After a minute, the saxophone player adjusted the mood once more, and slowed the tempo to a moderate, soulful song. Amanda sipped more of her soda, licking the moisture from her lips. Brandon still watched her, but now he was smiling. She remembered his smile from the day they met on the courts. He was so confident and attractive, evoking her trust even then, when he'd gentlemanly helped with her zipper.

Recalling her amusing first and last lesson, Amanda smiled back. No matter what they experienced together, she was always compelled to trust him. Even in the face of his mysterious past, she wasn't convinced that knowing the details mattered. Everyone had a past they didn't wish to share. Besides, she thought, after three weeks she'd seen no concrete evidence to support her father's judgments about Brandon.

The number ended and the audience clapped. "Thank you, Brandon," she said, seizing the moment of quietness. "This was a pleasant idea."

He gave a tender smile and reached to place his hand on hers. The warmth flowed beyond her hand and bathed her with inward calm.

"I'm glad to be here with you, Amanda."

The lead player thanked the crowd, and mentioned the band would be taking a break after the next song. Then he blew the beginning notes of "When a Man Loves a Woman." Several couples exchanged places on the dance floor.

"Amanda?" Brandon squeezed her palm.

She turned to look at him, seeing a tender yearning in his eyes.

"Dance . . . just one with me?"

Delaying her response, she questioned her intuition, but could find no warnings. All she saw was sincerity in his eyes. "All right," she said.

Brandon tipped the last of his drink, then stood to take her hand. He led her onto the darkened floor, not far from their table. There he turned and embraced her gently.

Wherever he brushed against her Amanda felt the kindled warmth of his body. Her adrenaline flowed as they swayed to the passionate tone of the sax. Brandon lifted his hand to brush hair from her face, and the delicate touch of his fingers left a tingling in her cheek.

In the dimly lit room, she met his steady gaze. Her loyalty to her father suddenly dove into a tailspin with her emotions trailing behind. Rationality seeped away, leaving her vulnerable to acute longings.

Brandon slowed his dancing and supported her neck with one hand, his watchfulness unchanging. She remembered his promise to remain distant. Businesslike. He'd said she'd have to come to grips with the truth about her feelings. He had told her—until then—that his actions would be strictly professional. Amanda had come to terms with her feelings for Brandon, but now she faced the driving need to prove them to him. No longer was she able to keep the distance between them. She wanted—needed—to love him.

The saxophone player started a crescendo, nearing the end of the song. He held an extended note. Amanda closed her eyes, raising up on her toes to kiss Brandon. Their lips met in a simple, soft press, but the contact changed rapidly to reflect passions inside. As though on cue with the band, they ended their kiss during the final notes. Brandon pulled back, looking surprised and pleased. He traced her lips with one finger.

"What was that?" he asked.

"I needed to do that," she said.

"I know." He smiled, tucking her head under his chin softly to lay her face against his chest. He hugged her tightly.

This feels so right, she mused. She closed her eyes, listening to the steady thump-thump of his heart, wishing the moment would never end.

"Want some fresh air?" he asked.

She gazed up at him, feeling like a puppy clutched in the protection of his arms. She nodded her agreement, and Brandon led her from the dark, overheated room into the cool air outside. They walked to his car and he leaned against it, reaching for her other hand. He looked eagerly at her and drew her close, kissing her again and again, until she had to withdraw for a breath. Then he held her.

Amanda heaved a sigh. A sigh of defeat? she wondered. No matter how hard she tried, she could never go long without being drawn to him. She'd clearly known it tonight, when they'd left the stables. She'd come willingly. Yet now she was forced to resolve how she would handle the situation with her father. Brandon was sure to expect some commitment.

"Amanda?" His warm breath drifted against her neck in the night air. He brushed his lips against her cheek and earlobe, causing her to shudder from his touch. "Come to the cabin with me, for the weekend?"

Air escaped her lungs. She hadn't expected this great a commitment, and she pulled away. His eyes revealed an honest yearning.

"I know you want to be with me. Come to the cabin. Just for the holiday. Give me a chance to—"

"I can't. I—I mean, I need to be at the publishing house tomorrow."

"Tomorrow? It's the Fourth of July. Only hospitals are open." He eyed her quizzically. "You aren't afraid of being alone with me, are you?"

He smiled, pulling her waist against him and nuzzling her ear. She winced. *Petrified* would be a better word.

Melting from his kisses, she pulled back again. "Yes. And I promised Mary I'd give her the day off."

"So what about tomorrow night? Are you booked up all weekend, or just avoiding saying yes? And I know you want to, so don't lie."

His playful manner lured her. She briefly considered his offer, but as Brandon drifted his lips along her shoulder she knew she could never take the risk of an overnight stay. "I don't know—"

"I won't accept no," he whispered, trailing his kisses farther down.

Running out of endurance, Amanda stopped him and pulled his chin up. "All right. *All right.* I'll drive down, but not until Sunday. And *only* for the day. I'm not staying overnight."

"Too bad. Sounds nice, hmm?"

"And don't think that you can change my mind," she asserted.

"Really? I bet I can change your mind, but I won't try to."

She breathed heavily, in awe of his influence. "I'm not going to argue anymore," she said. "It's late. I need to open by nine tomorrow morning."

"Mmmm. Guess I'll have to put my cravings on hold. But only for now."

As Brandon drove them back, Amanda leaned back against the headrest. He reached over to caress her cheek. Then he smiled. Sleepily, she smiled back.

They arrived at the stables and he walked her to her car. She slid in while he wrote out directions to the cabin.

"Here you go. I'll be waiting," he said huskily, hand-ing the paper to her. He leaned on her car door as she fastened her seat belt.

She wanted to say something, but a twinge of uncertainty knotted inside her. *Daddy.* She decided not to tell anyone where she'd be going on Sunday.

Driving home, Amanda tried reevaluating her situation with Brandon. Had things really changed between them, or did her passion ignite only because the mood had invited it? As she pulled into her home driveway, she concluded it was a combination of both. The romantic ambience had simply encouraged her to admit her true feelings. Now she had to decide what to do about them.

Amanda reviewed a long list, finishing the last few items. She'd already cleaned up the printing room and tidied up her father's office. She couldn't find much else to do on a holiday weekend, since the printers and editors were off. The print runs and shipments for the week were completed. She'd also returned the few calls for her father, and helped the only customer they'd had all morning in the shop's unique, small bookstore.

Glancing through yesterday's mail, Amanda sorted advertisements and flyers, and scanned the bills, leaving them for Benjamin. The rumbling in her empty stomach alerted her to the time. Seeing it was nearly one o'clock, she got her purse from the office and told Benjamin she would take her lunch.

She strolled in the warm sunshine. As she neared the center of town she heard lively bands passing a block away. Amanda joined the crowds to watch the fanfare of floats and marchers. Balloons and confetti filled the air. She loved parades. They were joyous and fun. They declared victory to the crowds. Today's jubilee symbolized independence from oppression. It made her heart squeeze. She knew she had yet to take that step. But she was ready. In her heart she determined now was the time to catch her dreams.

After watching for a half hour, the last of the floats passed and the crowds dispersed. Her stomach growled again and she moved on in search of food. As she walked, she reflected on the combined experience she'd received at her father's business and the stables. Her preliminary plans were organized. Research on facility costs were double-checked and the layouts for the grounds were finished. She'd even outlined the costs of her overhead and scaled them down to a minimum. Overall, she'd prepared a laudable start. Everything was ready, except . . . the horses. Her mother's endowment would adequately start the business and buy three horses, leaving her a reserve for emergencies and first-year expenses. However, she'd hoped to purchase six. Postponing the other three horses—along with the remaining talk with her father—was disheartening.

To add to her list of obstacles, she'd called Sam Finley and he'd found nothing about Brittany's name being removed from the list, except that it wasn't an error. Still, Amanda had to go on with her plans even if things didn't work out perfectly. And that meant with or without her father.

After lunch she returned and shooed Benjamin away

for his lunch, reassuring him she could handle whatever came up. He left eagerly.

Knowing the jingling bells above the door would alert her to any customers, she plopped onto the wood office chair. It creaked. Then silence poured into the room, engaging her thoughts back to Brandon. What would he be doing? She envisioned him lying in a hammock, swaying in the summer breeze. How nice it would be to crawl into the hammock with him, snuggle in his embrace, and—

Ring! The telephone beside her commanded her attention.

"Good afternoon. Huntington House . . . Benjamin? . . . He'll be back in an hour . . . Yes, I'll give him your number. Good-bye."

After Amanda penned the message and tore it from the carbon log, she leafed casually through the pad of yellow pages to pass time, curious as to what manner of business they did on a given day. The callers ranged from buyers, authors, agents, printing supply vendors, and deliveries. She read through Benjamin's scrawling penmanship, amazed at how intricate transactions could be in a small-time publishing house. She admired their system of marking all the calls that were returned, for later reference.

Leafing weeks back, Amanda saw a message that had gone unreturned—from Derrek Madison. She sat up in the chair. Checking days before it, she noticed a consistent pattern. His recurring efforts were flagrant, almost daily, from early June until the day her father left for London. All of them read the same message: *Important. Please return call.*

Amanda stared, mesmerized. Savage doubts darted through her mind. Brandon had been trying to contact Jonathan for weeks. She remembered Jonathan's mandate about having Brandon arrested if he persisted in "harassing" him. Was something so serious that Brandon would risk being arrested, just to talk to her father?

Continuing to scan the log, she was caught in a whirlwind of questions. But beyond early June she found no other calls from Derrek Madison. Bewildered, she flopped the log's pages back to her starting point.

The telephone rang again, jarring her already frenzied nerves. "Huntington House." Her curt reply sounded flat. Her efforts to sound cheerful had vanished.

"Jonathan Chambers, please," bellowed a stern, authoritative voice.

"I'm sorry. Mr. Chambers isn't available. May I take a message?"

"Certainly. This is Sgt. Hale at the Charlottesville Police Department. Please inform him that the department needs to discuss a matter with him regarding Derrek Madison, immediately upon his return, ma'am."

"Sgt. Hale, I'm afraid that will be some time. He's in London for a brief stay. I'm his daughter, Amanda Chambers. Is something wrong?"

"I apologize for the inconvenience, especially on a holiday, but this is a confidential matter, according to Mr. Madison. You understand."

Understand? She didn't understand any of this entangled mess, and it was infuriating when everyone sidestepped her pleas for clarification.

"Actually, I don't understand. If my father is in trouble, I believe I have a right to know, Sergeant."

"Sorry, Miss Chambers, but I'm only authorized to speak with him directly. Could you tell me where your father can be reached in London?"

"He's staying at the Park Lane Hotel, on Piccadilly."

"Thanks. I wish I hadn't missed him, but I'm a little late getting to this. Sorry to involve you, Miss Chambers. Have a nice day."

With his unceremonious good-bye, he hung up. Amanda sat in shock, the receiver clutched in her hand. *"Have a nice day?"* she spitefully recounted his words. Her mood suspended on the edge of fury and she slammed the receiver down, turning to fish through the message log.

"Where are those numbers? It's time I got to the heart of this." She ripped out a page to keep and show Brandon, once she reached the cabin. But in looking it over once more, it dawned on her that the number wasn't local but international—with a London prefix.

Glancing at her watch she saw it would be another forty-five minutes before Benjamin returned. Amanda dialed the Charlottesville library and asked them to look up the number for her in their reverse listing.

"Hello?" the librarian reappeared. "Yes, ma'am. Sorry to take so long. It's for Cordell Press in London. But there's a sublet in Virginia. Do you want that number too?"

"No . . . thank you." Numbly, Amanda ended the call, more questions escalating in her mind. Obviously, Brandon hadn't flown to London to try to contact her father.

Why, why, why? Amanda paced the wooden floors, her mind gyrating rapidly, rehashing everything that had transpired in the last four weeks.

"How could I have trusted him? He keeps so many secrets!" she said, venting her outrage. "He doesn't care about me. He's probably only using me to get back at

Father for that book," she blurted the words and halted her pacing.

"The book! Of course. Oh, Amanda, sometimes you are so naive. He's been trying to release a book. He must be releasing it from London." Now she eagerly paced the upstairs windows. "Oh, I wish Benjamin would come back."

Soon, Ben's blond head appeared around the corner and her wish was granted. She turned and grabbed her purse, then thundered down the staircase. The door opened, chiming the bells hung against it. Benjamin walked through munching a hot dog. His round-rimmed glasses rested on the end of his nose as he chomped. Yellow bangs draped his forehead, nearly covering his eyes.

"Benjamin! I am so glad you're back."

Surprise crossed his face. He shoved back the interfering flap of hair.

"I need your help. First, tell me what you know about this man who's been calling Daddy for weeks." She approached his six-foot-five frame and held the carbon message page up to his inquisitive face.

"Oh. Madison. Not much really. He's very persistent. Every time he calls I tell him Mr. Chambers doesn't want to talk to him. And each time the guy tells me to say it's important, that Jonathan should call that number."

"That's all?" Amanda winced, blinking.

"Yeh. Except that it really bothers your dad, Amanda. He's not himself after that guy calls. He's always really agitated. You know, red-faced and uptight?" Benjamin consumed another bite of his hot dog and wiped his face.

"I hate to even tell him when it's the same guy on the phone."

"I empathize completely," she said, knowing her father's moods. "What about the Charlottesville authorities—have they called before today?"

Benjamin had popped the last of his meal into his mouth and tried hard to swallow. "You mean *police*?" he squawked and slurped some of his cola to wash down the barrier of food. "No, I don't think so. Why?"

"Well, they called a few minutes ago. They wouldn't explain to me what they wanted, but they said it was a confidential matter with Derrek Madison."

"The police have never called as long as I've been here." He finished his drink and squinted his eyes. "You don't suppose your father's into some bad dealings, do you?" He pushed his round glasses up on his nose.

"No. My father is too proper for anything like that . . . I hope. It must be about a book." She glanced at the telephone number again. "I called the library and found this number is a London publishing house, owned by this man, *Madison.*" She blurted the name, repulsed by Brandon's secrets.

"I'm sorry, Amanda. I wish I knew more, but your father's very tight-lipped about this guy. Like I said, he only gets angry. He never talks about why the guy's calling all the time." Benjamin looked at her meekly. "What about trying the number, to find out why he's supposed to call?"

Amanda realized that she was encouraging disloyalty to his employer. She decided to curtail his involvement. "It's nightfall there. Tomorrow's no good either, because it's Sunday. I can't even try microfiche, without a title or a release date."

Benjamin nodded silently.

"I'm stuck until Monday. Dash it all! That will be too late."

"Late for what?"

"Tomorrow, I—" She stopped, feeling her cheeks turn hot. She couldn't even trust Benjamin with the knowledge that she was going to meet with "Mr. Madison." "Nothing. It's just that this whole thing is rather distressing."

"I'm sure it is." He regarded her sympathetically, looking over the rim of his circular-framed glasses.

"Say, Ben? Do you think you'd mind having the last few hours off? There haven't been two customers in the bookstore all day and everything for next week's deadlines has been finished."

"Fine by me. Don't worry, Amanda. I'm sure your father wouldn't do something . . . well, you know—illegal."

"I know. Thank you."

Relieved that Benjamin was agreeable to the time off, Amanda drove home, not willing to wait any longer to confront Brandon. He wouldn't be expecting her until tomorrow.

All the better, she thought affirmatively of her plan. She would catch him off guard for once.

Chapter Nine

Brandon's directions to the cabin were easy to follow. Amanda nursed her vengeance during the couple of hours of traveling the Blue Ridge highlands, not wanting to be influenced by his persuasive ways when she arrived. She made the last turn onto his gravel driveway. As the rays of afternoon light started to disappear behind the trees, she prepared to face Brandon.

Remember, you're definitely not staying—no matter how he tries to convince you, she coached herself, tossing her hot black hair from her shoulder, and wishing desperately she had the stamina to keep her decision.

She brought the car to a halt and looked the cabin over. It seemed deserted. Brandon's car was nowhere to be found. She stepped out to inspect things more closely, hoping he hadn't planned to stay out long. She peeked in the side windows. No one.

That was odd. Where could he be? Her long drive full of coaching did not entail the possibility of waiting around for him. She wondered when he'd be coming back, or if she'd be stuck there, until late in the evening.

The front door was unlocked, and Amanda let herself in. With the nonstop trip over, and the uneasiness of the empty house, she needed to use the bathroom. Afterward, she sauntered into the living room, observing Brandon's newly moved-in, exorbitantly expensive furniture. She viewed the black leather couch, big-screen television, original oil paintings, and sleek tribal rug.

Growing anxious, she walked down the hall and peeked in his bedroom, as much from curiosity as boredom. He hadn't shown her this room when she visited before. She walked through the master bedroom, noticing the king-size bed. Beside it were weight sets, taking up half of the room's space. Then she wandered into the private bathroom, well lit by a huge skylight and decorated with a forest of ferns, philodendrons, and African violets. Its bleach-white tiling and walls were aesthetically coordinated with midnight-blue colored towels, rugs, shower curtain, and accessories. But she gasped at what impressed her the most: the large, sunken Jacuzzi tub. The thought of a bath sounded wonderful right now, but she couldn't risk it.

Leaving his room, Amanda passed the spare bedroom, still without a spare bed. Only a rolltop desk graced the room. On the built-in bookshelf, numerous volumes were now shelved. She scanned the titles and recalled the many books in his office at the club. As she moved from one shelf to the next, she realized most of the authors were all the same. B.D. Madison.

"Naturally. Brandon Derrek Madison." she whispered. "And all by Cordell Press." Unearthing the books refueled her tumultuous feelings about the phone calls. She leafed through several, reading the backs. All of them had that certain trait of an exposé.

"Repulsive," she said seethingly, shoving one back in its slot on the shelf. Then she frowned, feeling pity for her father. For whatever reason, he didn't deserve to become party to someone's vicious, money-making publication, and if Brandon really cared about her, he wouldn't go through with it.

An hour passed. Still no Brandon. Tired of reading, she glanced around, spying a London telephone book on the desk next to her. Amanda reached for it and searched for Cordell Press. It was listed, just as she expected, but what surprised her was the address.

"It can't be! That's Jillian's, in London." Amanda felt dizzy. The more she discovered, the more confused and suspicious she became. Maybe Daddy was right. Maybe Brandon really was threatening him. She again wondered how she could have trusted someone who had so much to hide.

Amanda heard a door close. Startled by the sudden noise she dropped the telephone book. The volume collapsed onto the floor in a crumpled heap. She swiftly retrieved it, smoothed out the pages, and slid it onto the desk. But she accidentally knocked the pencil cup over and sent pencils rolling across the desktop. She scrambled for the pencils, replacing them in the cup. Not wanting to reveal that she'd been snooping, she tiptoed to the hallway door to see if she could spot Brandon.

She checked the living room. He wasn't there. Nor the

kitchen. He had just walked in and disappeared. She went to check the den. Without windows it was too black to see, so she reached for the light switch.

Someone suddenly grabbed her arm, pulled her into the darkness, and covered her head with a towel. They tossed her onto the floor and forcefully sat on top of her, pressing the air from her lungs. Amanda wasn't even sure if it was Brandon, and in her fright she flailed her arms and kicked, trying to scream with what breath she had, but the towel muffled her attempts.

"Come to rip off my house, huh? Well, you messed with the wrong man."

"Brandon!" she shrieked. "Wait!"

"What the—? *Amanda?*" Brandon's voice held genuine surprise, and he stripped off the towel, rising at once to throw on the light switch.

"Yes, it's me!" she exploded.

"What are you doing here?"

"You invited me. Remember?" She was still on her back, sprawled upon the wood floor, lacking the wind to sit up just yet. "And just whose BMW did you think was parked in the drive?"

"I came in the back way. I didn't see the car. I heard a noise, so I thought you were a prowler." He stood gaping at her. "I wasn't expecting you until tomorrow, you know," he said in defense of his actions.

Amanda turned to scowl at him, and he extended a hand to help her up. She didn't accept and stood on her own, dusting herself off. Her abundant, sable hair fell in mussed heaps and she attempted to smooth it out.

"We have had burglars roaming around," he continued. "They've hit up several houses not too far from here."

"Right," she spat a reply. "That's why you left your door unlocked?"

"Force of habit, I guess. It never had a lock until I decided to move in. There wasn't much to take, before. I forgot, since I left the back way."

The words bounced off Amanda. She was still very sore from being pounced on, not to mention her wounded pride.

"Come on, I'll pour you a drink. I could sure use one after the way you scared me."

"Scared *you?*" she raged. "Who was knocked violently to the floor and nearly suffocated by a towel?"

"You know, you're really enchanting when you're hopping mad."

She threw him a harsh glare and Brandon broke into laughter.

"All right. I'm sorry I frightened you. Truce?"

With his piecemeal apology, she resigned her outrage and followed him into the kitchen, sitting at the kitchen bar. Brandon poured two gingerales. Amanda tasted the fizzing concoction, and drank in a good portion of the cool liquid to relieve her parched throat.

"How'd you drive up and not see the BMW?"

"I didn't drive. I walked. Through a trail behind the house, the other direction. I blazed it when the house was built. It runs all the way to the main road, and town is only a mile further."

"Where's your car?"

"Had to take it in and have my brakes checked. The

garage is only five miles away with the trail, so I walked home. It was good exercise.''

Amanda finished her drink and could feel her sore muscles relaxing.

''So why did you come today, Amanda?''

Her muscles tensed. She looked up at him, contemplating her answer. Ever since she'd heard Brandon return home, she'd forgotten her quest. *And to think I'm having a congenial drink with him,* she chided herself. She couldn't believe her well-planned strategy had been so overturned by circumstances, and she pushed away from the bar, trying to put some distance between them.

''I came to get some answers, Brandon. Today the authorities called for my father. You know, the police? You wouldn't happen to know anything about that, would you?'' She faced him again.

His expression turned somber, but he didn't reply.

''Well, the sergeant claimed the call was initiated by you.'' She watched him, enjoying holding the reigns in the argument for once.

''What'd they say?'' he asked, leaving the kitchen and approaching the huge picture windows in the living room.

''Nothing. Absolutely nothing. 'This is a strictly confidential matter, according to Mr. Madison . . . you understand.' '' she mimicked the sergeant's words, still profoundly colored by her own British accent. Brandon stared out the windows, into the fading light of early evening.

''And that's not all. I found your messages, Brandon. All thirteen of them. All marked IMPORTANT. Now what is going on? You keep telling me that I should trust you, but when I see evidence like this mounting up against you, causing me to doubt you instead, I—I think you're lying to me.''

"You're not going to like what I have to say, Amanda.'' He paused, finally turning to her. "This wouldn't have happened if your father wasn't such a stubborn man.''

"It takes one to know one!'' she snapped.

"Yes, I'm obstinate too,'' he voiced his disturbance. "Especially, when it comes to matters as precious as you.'' He zeroed his intense gaze at her eyes and then he returned to the kitchen, sipping his drink.

"Don't try to flatter me, Brandon. I don't believe you have my best interests at heart anymore. I'm not certain you ever have.'' She hoped it wasn't true, but she had to pin down some answers. "Now, tell my why you're harassing my father or I'm going to call the police.''

Brandon opened his mouth to talk, but stopped abruptly, pounding his glass upon the countertop. It sloshed and fizzed over with bubbles. Amanda shuddered. She hadn't foreseen pushing him to the breaking point.

"I can't tell you everything, but I'll tell you *why*.'' He pointed his finger at her. "Because your sweet, wonderful father doesn't want you to know. That's right. And, like a fool, I promised him I'd let him do the explaining, firsthand. But now it's going to be too late.''

Amanda's adrenaline raced as she digested his words. For the first time, she admitted her father *could* be in serious trouble. That would explain why everyone was upset and trying to keep the details from her.

"What do you mean, it will be too late? Because of that horrible book you wrote about him? Is that why?"

"I haven't written any books."

"How can you lie like that? They are stacked in your spare room—B.D. Madison—shelves of lives torn apart by your scandal-laden publications."

Brandon's expression turned severe. "Those books were not written by me," he spoke forcefully, retaining his control.

"No? Then who is B.D. Madison?" she said jeeringly.

"My father."

"What?"

"Yes, Amanda, my father, Brandon Derrek Madison, the first, wrote those books. I'm the second, and proud to follow in his footsteps with the publishing house, but I've never written any books. And as for whether those books should be put to shame for revealing scandals, my dad uncovered many an illegal operation—all for the good of humanity—all to improve the livelihoods of innocent people who were severely endangered by others." His voice was rising. "He wrote to uphold the morale of the public and to reveal the truth, dispelling delusions other newspapers were satisfied to print."

"And he just happened to write the book you tried to involve my father in? Your father is dead, Brandon. Just how did he write that one?" She crossed her arms, waiting.

"He wrote it last year, before he died, and he asked me to see that it was published when I took over the business."

"You . . . you're going to publish it, aren't you?" Realization stung her like a venomous bite. "No matter how it might destroy my father? No matter what filth you spread over me and my family?''

''It won't happen like that, Amanda. Please, trust me.''

''*Trust you?* A master of charades?'' Tears streamed down her face. ''You're not worth it!'' she wailed, and ran from the house.

Stumbling toward her car, Amanda grabbed for the door handle but it only flipped. She yanked twice more, vainly. Horrified, she peered inside the shadowy interior. Her fear was true. The keys dangled from the ignition.

''Bloody automatic doors!'' she swore, losing the remainder of her self-control. She slunk down onto the gravel to lean back against the tire. There she buried her face in her arms to sob.

After her wail, she felt Brandon's hand rest on her head.

''Just—leave me—alone.''

''Amanda . . . I'll help you get your keys.''

''I don't want your help,'' she mumbled. ''I don't want you!''

''Yes, you do,'' he coaxed her serenely, kneeling beside her. ''You know that as plainly as those keys are in that car. You're upset because of what's happened, and you have a right to be. Everything makes me look suspicious. That's why I asked you to follow your heart from the beginning.''

She kept her head buried, trying to quell her emotions.

''Besides,'' he continued, ''if I'd honestly wanted to cause you harm, don't you think I've had enough chances by now?'' He laughed softly. ''It's a good thing I'm not as sinister as you think.''

She looked at him, sniffling. "I want proof."

"About your dad?"

She looked intently at him, hungering for valid information.

Brandon frowned. "He's the only one who can give you that. And I'm not holding back because I want to, Amanda. I gave him my word, to wait."

She realized the restraint in him. He had to keep something from her that he'd rather not.

"You go clean up and I'll find a coat hanger to get your keys."

Not so reluctantly, she went inside to wash up in the guest bathroom. She flicked on the light and winced. Mascara had run ghastly black streaks and smudges beneath her now-bloodshot blue eyes.

"Hideous!" She gasped and turned on the faucet. She freshened up, chilling the swollen areas around her eyes with a cold washcloth, then she went back to see how Brandon was managing with her keys. But on the way out, he called her from the couch.

"You have them already?"

"Afraid not." He looked at her matter-of-factly.

"What? You said—"

"Yes, I said I would get them for you, but I couldn't. That's a newer model. The window's too tight to slip the hanger in. The only other way would be to smash the window. Or, we can call a locksmith in the morning."

"*Morning?*"

"Well, which is it? I've got a sledgehammer in the garage. That ought to work. Or, can you manage to stand being around me for one evening?"

Brandon looked dead serious, but in the irony of the situation Amanda started laughing. A wry grin covered his face as she broke into hilarity.

"What's so funny?" he asked, tilting an eyebrow.

Finally managing to catch her breath Amanda explained the source of her amusement. "When I drove here I swore that nothing—positively nothing—would make me stay overnight." Overtaken by laughter again, she was no longer able to speak, and slumped onto the leather couch beside him.

He shook his head and slipped his arm around her shoulders. "And now you're stuck here for twelve hours. What a shame," he teased her.

The glint in Brandon's eyes grabbed her attention and she caught the playful tone of his voice. "It is rather funny," she admitted, trying to suppress the laughing spell as the hue in his eyes darkened to blue-violet.

"Well, I'm sure we'll find something to do together." He ran a finger lightly across the back of her hand, gazing at her for a moment. Then he stood and walked to the kitchen.

She recalled their episode in the parking lot at the club, how he'd tried changing her mind, kissing her enticingly until she pushed him away. Was she really prepared to spend an evening with him in the same house? She bit her lower lip, feeling her amusement seep away.

"Ready for dinner?" he called from the kitchen. "I'm starved. That five-mile hike made me hungry." He browsed around in the cupboards, clanging pots and clinking dishes, then running a jet of water.

He cooks? This I have to see, she thought, intrigued. She joined him in the kitchen and sat at the bar again, squishing into the cozy, leather stool seat. "I ate something about four-thirty, but maybe I could have an apple?"

"An apple?" Brandon quipped, and without answering her request he started cracking eggs one-handed into a bowl, and adding milk with the other.

She watched, amused by his gourmet demonstration. "Do you cook often?"

"Have to. I live alone. I can't stand fast food and restaurants aren't my thing. I like homemade meals." He grabbed some fresh mushrooms and Jack cheese from the refrigerator.

"Well, you could hire a cook."

"Nah." After grating the cheese, Brandon sliced a few mushrooms and spread the ingredients over the bubbling mixture. He added dashes of salt and pepper. "I like to know what's in my food."

He folded the omelet and dished it onto a plate. Amanda smelled the cheese-and-mushroom aroma. Her stomach growled. "That smells delicious."

"Want a bite?"

"Well . . . all right."

Brandon cut a piece and after blowing to cool it, he lifted it into her mouth. "Whoops!" He grabbed his napkin and dabbed at the sauce trailing down her chin.

"Mmm. That's wonderful. Much better than mine."

"*You* cook?" He looked surprised.

"Well, I've tried. But it never turns out as tasty as that."

Brandon smiled, turning to the fridge and opening the door wide to browse. Amanda saw that the bottom shelf was filled with a number of corked and foil-topped bottles. He selected one and set it on the counter, noticing her surprise. "Sparkling cider."

"I see. Do you have your own orchard?"

He gave her a lopsided grin, slipped in the corkscrew, and popped the cork with ease. Then he retrieved two goblets, and as he poured the amber liquid, it gurgled from the bottle into the cut-crystal glasses. He raised her a glass and Amanda took it, brushing his fingers in the exchange. Feeling a little giddy, she watched him closely.

"A toast," he said optimistically.

"To what?"

"To . . . wine, women, and song."

Amanda rolled her eyes. "I can't drink to that!"

He stopped grinning and looked at her sincerely, expectantly. "To us."

She could see flecks of violet enhancing his blue eyes.

"I can think of nothing better than having you by my side, Amanda."

She enjoyed his tender compliment and raised her glass. "To us."

They clinked rims and mutually drank in a swallow. The tangy flavor bit Amanda's taste buds, and she grimaced, making a sour face. "This doesn't go too well with omelets."

Brandon chuckled. "The first swallow will clear your palate. Try another sip."

She drank in another swallow. "Umm. You're right." The cider's flavor converted to a more mellow, pleasant one, sending a glow through her.

"Just takes getting used to," he said.

"Yes." She mentally compared the cider's effects to

Brandon: *Comes on strong and then pacifies you with gentleness.*

He smiled affectionately, momentarily avoiding his meal, and then resumed his interest with another portion of egg and cheese.

"What are you thinking about?" she ventured.

He swallowed. "That it's nice to have companionship out here. I'm not looking forward to living alone in this huge place."

"You're living here already?" She hadn't expected to sound so surprised, but the thought of him being so far away knotted her stomach.

"Soon. My condo sold yesterday. I'll be out before August."

Amanda wasn't sure why she felt so sullen, but she hadn't realized that his move would come so soon.

Finishing his omelet, he turned to the sink and rinsed his plate. Then he put the remaining food away and turned off the kitchen light. "Man, it's hot in here." He stripped off his T-shirt and came around to her side. "Let's go sit on the deck and catch that gorgeous sunset."

Amanda inhaled sharply, astounded by the contours of his bared chest with its patch of curly brown hair. Each muscle was defined. She sat motionless on the stool, unable to take her eyes off of him. He took her by the hand and clutched the bottle of cider, leading them both out to the deck.

Once outside in the cooler air, Amanda set down her glass on the lacquered-wood patio table, and gazed at the glowing sunset. She leaned against the deck's railing, breathing in the dogwood-scented air. Brandon approached and leaned against the railing next to her.

"It's lovely," she praised the sky's rosy and fiery-tinged grandeur.

"Once I saw those Virginia sunsets, I never wanted to live anywhere else."

"I love to watch the sunset. I've done so for several years."

"Good for you." He watched her admiringly. "Most people don't know how to appreciate such beauty."

"I did it to dream, mostly. It was a place where I could go to be alone with my thoughts, and sort out my problems. A kind of therapy I got into the habit of, after the accident."

"What accident?"

Amanda glanced at him, realizing she'd never explained. Taking in a deep breath, she began narrating her sordid tale.

"I had a riding accident when I was young. I got caught in the middle of a beastly rainstorm." Seeing his interest, she continued. "It happened about a year after I learned to ride. I went to the stables every weekend and I knew those grounds thoroughly, but when the storm hit it was so terrible that I couldn't see in front of me. I collided with a low tree branch and it knocked me off my horse. I was unconscious for a couple of hours, according to the paramedics. Evidently, the horse made it back to the stables without me and they started a search. I was in a sorry state when they found me, all bruised and broken—soaked to the bone and chilled from the freezing rain."

"That's awful. You must have been terrified."

"I was, at first. But after healing from the accident, I faced a larger tragedy. All I wanted to do with my life was to own horses and eventually run a stable business. But after the accident my father told me—in no uncertain terms—that I was never going riding again. I was shattered. I didn't know what else to do. Mother told me to give it time. She always encouraged me, saying, 'Your wounds healed with time, and your father's will too.' "

"But he's still against it."

"Yes. Every time I broached the topic, he grew more resistant. Mother tried to help convince him, but he was just too shaken by the accident to let go of his fears. That's why I started ballet lessons. They were his idea, and I thought it would be best to make him happy for a while. Then I would approach him later with my idea, when I was older."

"Have you tried since then?"

"Sort of. But within the next year after his refusals, I lost my mother to leukemia . . . exactly at sunset. Everything changed then. I didn't want to upset him further with the issue and decided to wait. For years I told myself Mother was right. Someday he would change his mind."

"Do you think it's still possible?"

She looked to Brandon. His expression was so serious. "Yes. For some strange reason, I believe it's still possible. Father and I finally came to an understanding on the issue of riding. Yet, when I tried discussing the stable idea with him, he gave me a long discourse about the unreliability of owning a business, and how horses were unprofitable nonsense."

"Jonathan's inflexible when it comes to hearing something he doesn't want to."

"Yes, he . . . is." She studied him, wondering just how well Brandon knew her father. "Anyway, he probably assumes I've forgotten the whole thing. But I'm not giving up. I have everything ready. I'm prepared to move out, if necessary, and look for other partners if he's not in favor of the idea."

Brandon paused. He smiled. He went in the house and returned, lighting two sparklers. He handed one to her. "Happy Independence Day, Amanda."

She smiled and took the sparkler. As it crackled downward and then fizzled out she felt changed. Burdens that she'd carried for years were suddenly lifted. Gone. For the first time in a long time, she felt free.

The skylight had transformed into a violet-pink as the final rays of color were absorbed by the dusk. Amanda finished her drink, and felt drained from the exasperating day. She sat down on the patio chair's ottoman and craned her neck from side to side, stretching out sore muscles.

"Long day, huh?" Brandon spoke softly.

She rubbed at her neck, enjoying the soothing effect his deep voice had on her. "Actually, I think you were the culprit—yanking me onto the floor with a towel wrapped around my head. Not exactly a warm welcome."

"Sorry. I do know a better one."

In the faint light of dusk she saw his face brimming with desire. He crossed over to sit in the chair behind her and began rubbing her neck, kneading the soreness away. His rhythmic massage loosened the knot in her muscles, but planted one in the pit of her stomach.

Don't let him do it. Amanda. Don't let your defenses down, her logic entreated. But against the pacifying massage, her inner voice could have been screaming and still wouldn't have been heard. She yielded to his masterful hands, enjoying the comforting aid they brought her.

After a long time, she felt like jelly. She opened her eyes. Evening now darkened the sky and it grew dotted with the twinkling of stars.

Brandon pulled her against his chest, wrapping his arms securely around her. "Time for bed," he cooed, and effortlessly lifted her into his arms.

"Hmm?" She tried rising from his warm body.

"You can't stay awake all night. You have big, beautiful eyes, but they're not an owl's. And they've been closed for ten minutes. Come on."

"But—" She rubbed her eyes, struggling to revive herself.

"Stop worrying, Amanda. I'll sleep on the couch. You can have my bed all to yourself. For now."

Chapter Ten

Brandon brought Amanda into the master bedroom and switched on the light. "Too bright," she said as she shielded her eyes from the glare.

"No lights? Okay." He shut them off again, and placed her on the bed. Then he fished in the dark for a clean T-shirt. Placing the shirt in her hand, Brandon kissed her on the cheek. His warm lips enticed her mouth. "You have three minutes to get under the covers before I come back to tuck you in."

Amanda heard the door latch and sleepily started to undress. She fidgeted with the T-shirt, trying to find the neckline, and finally managed. It felt cool and soft. It smelled of fresh laundry soap, and a hint of Brandon's aftershave. Its freshness made her mouth raise into a smile.

She pulled back the covers and slipped into the bed,

yawning, growing drowsier with every minute. *Why do I always melt under his touch?* she mused. She lay motionless, drifting in a half-dreamy state, wondering about all the feelings welling inside of her and floating through her mind. As the sleepiness overshadowed her thoughts, everything muddled into one answer . . . "Because I love him," she breathed, barely above a whisper.

Amanda could smell bacon and coffee. She pried open one eye but the room was hazy and unclear. "Yum." She groaned. "Breakfast smells wonderful, Sara." Then she bolted into an upright position. "Sara!" she shrieked. "Oh, no! I forgot to call." She rushed out of the bedroom to find Brandon, without giving a thought to her appearance.

"Brandon? Where's the telephone?" She found him in the kitchen, his dark hair wet and slicked back. He hummed to himself in a smokey-gray, silk bathrobe with tiny red flecks splayed on the material. He turned and paused to look at her. He grinned.

" 'Morning, princess. And how's my sleeping beauty this morning?" He returned to humming, flipping bacon and popping bread into the toaster.

Amanda whirled around in circles looking frantically for the telephone. "Brandon, I need to use the—" At last, she looked down at herself and gasped, seeing the T-shirt too short for comfort, revealing her long legs. Dashing into the bedroom to change into her clothes, she looked everywhere for them, but they were gone. Frustrated, she grabbed the checkered quilt to wrap around her waist. Amanda waddled back into the kitchen, wishing the blanket would also cover her embarrassment.

"Where're my clothes?" She nudged onto a stool, keeping herself wrapped.

"In the dryer."

"What ever for?"

"Because I washed them last night. I needed to do a load of towels and I figured you wouldn't mind having them clean for today." He poured some orange juice into two small glasses.

"Oh." She was strangely pleased with his helpful initiative. "So, where do you hide the telephone?"

He pointed to the wall beside her and continued his cheerful humming as he sliced cantaloupe into bite-size pieces.

Amanda looked at the wall. The phone hung in plain view. She snatched the receiver and dialed home, letting it ring over and over. "Oh, where could she be? It's almost nine." Amanda replaced the receiver.

"Trying to call Sara?"

"Yes. I never called last night to tell her I wouldn't be coming home. All she knows is that I was going out for dinner with a friend. She'll be worried sick."

"No, she won't," Brandon poured her a mug of steaming coffee. "Cream?"

"She most certainly—"

"No, she won't, because I've already talked to her. Last night."

Amanda felt her face drain of its blood and she was certain she'd been shot—the pain in her chest felt genuine.

"You did *what?*" she shrieked.

"Calm down. I told her you came for dinner and had

car trouble, and that you'd be home in the morning after we got you on the road again.''

Amanda sensed the sustained pause while she recovered from her astonishment.

''In fact, I think she likes me. She remembered me from the party, and said how kind it was for me to put you up for the evening. Cream?''

''I can't believe you told her.'' Amanda grumbled at the invasion of her private affairs.

Brandon gave her a wry grin. ''I didn't exactly say you were sleeping in my bed. Besides, someone had to tell her something. You said yourself she'd be worried sick, and you were fast asleep, so I called.'' He poured cream in her mug, not waiting any longer for her answer.

Why did every problem have such a simple solution when Brandon was around? Staring blankly at her coffee, the answer from last night flooded into her mind again . . . *Because I love him.* She blinked in dismay. Had she spoken the words or was the confession part of her dreams? She couldn't differentiate between the two. She looked at Brandon sheepishly. He was grinning, setting two places at the bar for their breakfast, and still humming.

''Brandon? Last night, when you came in to get my clothes . . . was I . . . talking . . . in my sleep?''

''Do you talk in your sleep?'' He showed a feigned look of shock and Amanda scowled. ''Hmm—let me think. Oh, yes. Something about—what was it you said exactly? 'Because I love him'? Yeah, that was it.'' He dished up their meals and sat at the bar beside her, watching her closely.

Amanda felt heat rush into her face.

"But I don't think you were asleep yet," he added.

"I must have been." She looked away.

"No, because when I kissed you and tucked you in after that, you said 'Good-night, Brandon.' No, I'm sure you weren't asleep yet." He unfolded a napkin for his lap and, not waiting for her to recover from the shock, he unfolded another one for her, laying it on the quilt over her lap.

Amanda slowly turned to face him, dazed. "I thought I was dreaming when I said that."

"You weren't." He smiled and kissed her on the nose. She closed her eyes at the contact and, in the closeness, caught a whiff of his leathery cologne. The smooth smell further depleted her self-control. She swallowed. She thought how wonderful it would be to spend every morning with him.

"Eat your breakfast. You said nothing that I didn't already know."

When they'd finished eating, Brandon cleared their plates. "I'll need to install a dishwasher now that I'm going to be here all the time."

The looming reality upset her. "Your lessons must not be much longer."

"My last one is September first. But I'll have all my things moved here before the end of July. I'll commute until my last day, and then collect what's left in my office." Brandon slipped away to get dressed.

Amanda felt her throat tighten. Somehow she didn't want to accept his absence from her life. She was finally learning to trust him and accept the way he always stayed in control, but beyond that, she had confessed that she loved him . . . and Brandon had heard.

He reappeared, brawnily clad in weathered denim shorts and a maroon cotton shirt that hugged the contours of his chest.

He was even devastating in worn-out jeans. Brandon sat beside her to put on his socks. His hair was dry now, except for the back curls.

"Time to get my car and find a locksmith open on Sundays."

"What about my clothes?"

"Should be done in twenty minutes. I'll call after I pick up my car to let you know what I find out. Make yourself at home."

He looked at her affectionately and his tenderness tugged on her heart. She thought he was going to kiss her good-bye, as though she were his wife. Oddly, she already felt like it was home.

Brandon left through the back door, setting off for his five-mile hike. Cozying herself on the couch, Amanda glanced at a tennis magazine, flipping through the glossy pages. She glanced at the advertisements for rackets, shoes, gear, and clubs to join in the northeast area. It was hard for her to imagine Brandon giving up tennis and his club amenities altogether. But he was definitely moving.

With him out of the house it was safe to use the Jacuzzi undisturbed. Amanda took a long bath. The clothes dryer buzzed as she soaked, and after a while she reluctantly got out. After she dressed, she folded the other clean items, including some of Brandon's clothes. A grin spread on her face as she piled them into a neat stack. Even folding the man's clothes made her giddy.

Knowing her mind was drifting again, she decided to

take a walk outside in the warm July morning, and see more of the surroundings that she'd missed on her first visit. Turning the corner beyond the backyard she followed a different trail and stared in amazement. Brandon had built a tennis court, complete with a surrounding chain-link fence. Beside the court, the grounds were staked off and dug deeply for a swimming pool, and a diving board lay next to several bags of cement. In between the pool area and the court a large cedar gazebo had also been erected. The newly shingled structure was varnished to protect its wood from weathering.

She laughed. "So! He's *not* giving up his clubhouse luxuries."

After roaming through the gazebo she walked further down the path. It wound along a thin trail, bordered with trees, for about sixty or seventy feet. She knew it wasn't the same path that led down to the creek that they had taken last time, and her curiosity sparked. She wondered what else Brandon had been busy doing. Coming to the path's boundary she saw a steep drop-off and realized she was standing on a cliff. Brandon had cleverly taken advantage of the scenery by constructing a fenced lookout with large beams. Off to the side, there was a rocking love seat. Its perfect positioning near the edge of the cliff overlooked the valley, and the hills beyond were majestically draped in velvety blue-green shades.

Amanda sat in the love seat and gently rocked, swaying while her thoughts lingered on the peaceful view. Brandon had so much land it made her envious, wishing for such a beautiful place to operate her stables. Her father's land was adequate, but it was relatively flat and lacked the character of this hilly land bordering the Blue Ridge mountains.

After enjoying the scenery, she went back indoors to await Brandon's call. Time passed in silence, so she decided to find a book to read while she waited. She perused his bookshelves for the second time, but couldn't find anything to suit her tastes. "All these books and not one fiction." There were no novels, only the volumes by Brandon's father and various other nonfiction. Discouraged, she retreated to the den. Maybe he kept them separated? She checked each shelf, but the same was true. "Incredible." She slumped onto the den couch, crossing her arms. "How could a publisher, with a father who was a publisher, *not* have any fiction?"

She drummed her nails. Clicking echoed in the room. She stared blankly at the oak desk until, gradually, a galley proof came into focus.

An uneasy chill slithered through her spine. Amanda reached for the galley, reading the title with apprehension. "*Freedoms of the Press,*" she mumbled. Although her heart didn't want to look, she opened the cover and turned to the center where pages were bookmarked by a photograph. She looked at the photo curiously. Brandon—much younger, lankier, and without a tan—stood with his sister and some other fellow. All three had interlocked arms upon shoulders, a definite portrayal of closeness. But as she studied the other gentleman with his skinny frame, stocky jaw and wiry appearance, his features roused her memory with a vengeance—

"Mick Terrence! The scoundrel," she said in a rage.

Amanda then recognized the picture was taken in England, in front of her father's old employer. The Jillian's

Press sign could be partially seen in the background.

"Why on earth would Brandon be buddies with Mick Terrence?" Fear started clawing her insides again. *How well did she really know Brandon?* The telephone rang on the end table beside her, jangling Amanda as well as the silence. She took a deep breath, then answered on the third ring.

"Hello?"

"Hi, it's me. Amanda? You sound faint. Is everything okay?"

"Y-Yes. I was startled by the telephone, that's all." She examined the picture, wishing it held more answers.

"Sorry I took so long to call. My car's ready and I finally reached a locksmith. He's going to follow me back. I should be there in a half hour. I'd like for us to have some lunch before you head back, though, if that's all right with you? There's something I need to talk to you about."

Amanda felt paralyzed. She certainly wouldn't get very far discussing the book on the telephone—so she'd wait. "All right," was all she could utter, and Brandon said good-bye.

She replaced the receiver and stared at the photo. Then she began reading the chapter in the galley proof where the picture had been inserted. A whole chapter committed to Jillian's. Astounded, she read each word. She saw Terrence's name numerous times. He was made out to be a white-collar thief, stealing money from the house, laundering tens of thousands of pounds for himself.

She read on. Occasionally, her father's name appeared, but in context he was mentioned as somewhat of an innocent bystander. Although, the end of the chapter alluded to the idea that Jonathan knew more than he was telling—whether or not his knowledge implicated him along with Terrence—and that London officials should have investigated the matter more thoroughly. It made reference to the earlier trial, and quoted that ''certain people felt Jonathan Chambers left the country quietly, not wanting to face a retrial.''

Amanda hadn't even heard of the first trial. Her father had kept everything quiet. ''So that's what Terrence meant the night he called,'' she mumbled, still absorbing the sudden insight. Now that she finally knew the secrets, she wished they could be erased forever from her mind.

The crunching of tires on the gravel drive alerted her to Brandon's return. She went to the spare bedroom window to see. Sure enough, he was back with the locksmith, who in two minutes pulled the keys from her car's ignition. She watched Brandon pay the man, then turn to come in the house. She shivered, not wanting to thrash out the dreadful subject once again. However, now that she knew about the book there wasn't much he could be keeping from her. The locksmith drove away and she heard the front door open and shut.

''Amanda?'' he called from the foyer.

''Right here,'' she said, leaning against the bedroom doorjamb, watching him from down the hall. She had her arms crossed and knew the book was hidden from his sight, behind her back.

''There you are.'' He approached her with a smile. ''Your keys.'' He dangled them in her face. ''What's wrong? I got back as soon as I could. Are you hungry?''

His eyes revealed genuine concern, and Amanda was

feeling her feet turn cold about approaching the whole matter. She moved to take the keys with her free hand when she accidentally dropped the book and the picture slid out in plain view.

She watched him acknowledge the stray items on the floor, and his jaw muscles tightened. A lion couldn't have had a more powerful clench. She panicked as he reached down to recover his things. Then he faced her, obviously discerning the situation. He said nothing, but the angry look in his eyes questioned her silently.

Chapter Eleven

Amanda remained paralyzed and tongue-tied at the doorjamb, timidly glancing at Brandon and then down at the book.

"You've kept busy," he said finally. His tone was curt, unkind.

Still speechless, she conjured enough courage to nod her head.

"Well, now you know, Amanda. I wasn't going to tell you, but you found out anyway." He groaned from frustration. "I always knew it'd be too hard to keep this from you. But your father insisted." Brandon shoved at his hair, pushing it back in a feathered profile.

"Why?" She choked on the word, trying to hold back tears.

"He probably didn't want to spoil his impeccable image in your mind."

"But this book only claims he *may* have knowledge about laundering, and not direct involvement." She looked to him, confused, wanting answers.

Brandon strode from the living room, leaving Amanda to trail. "That's what we thought too." He tossed the galley ungraciously onto the kitchen counter with a *thwap*. Crossing the room, he glared out the windows.

"We?" she queried, following him.

"The police."

"Oh, that's right. The police. And I suppose they called yesterday because they also think he's innocent?" she said, chiding him.

"Yes, they *do*." He glowered at her, then back out the window. "The problem was they called too late and spoke to you."

"You know about the trial Mick Terrence is at?"

"Know?" He gave a gruff laugh. Sliding open the glass door, he walked onto the porch, leaving the passage open for her.

She followed, preparing herself for the unveiling of Brandon's story.

"I'm the one who got the local reporters going. I purchased Jillian's after you and your father moved here. I knew about my father's work on it in his latest book. After the first trial the business was steadily going downhill. So I changed the name."

"That's why Cordell Press was listed in London, with Jillian's address?"

"Exactly. The acquisition actually saved the business from ruin. Though I admit I had personal reasons for getting my hands on it."

"To convict my father of being more than innocent?"

"No." He glared. "To convict Mick Terrence . . . of murder."

"Murder!" She was jolted, taken back by the word.

"That's right. When Mick Terrence started his scam ten years ago we were friends." As Brandon relayed the account, venomous hatred poured from his lips. "We went to university in London together. I worked for my father and he worked for Jillian's. One day I waited for him to get off work so we could go out. I walked in the office and stumbled onto what he was doing."

"What did you see?"

"Everything. Paperwork, phony receipts, books. I confronted him with it as soon as he came back to the car, but he said he didn't know what I was talking about, that all that paperwork belonged to Jonathan."

"And you believed him?"

"Initially, but later that night I figured, if that was true, why wasn't your father around? I didn't have to wait long to get an answer. The next night I was almost murdered, and . . . " Brandon looked away, and his hesitation seemed provoked by emotion. "That's when they killed Jeannie, instead of me."

"You're sure the killer worked for him?"

"Positive. I also knew I had to leave town or he would try again. I called my father that night from the airport, and explained everything to him. I relocated in America, had my name legally changed to Brandon Cordell so they couldn't trace me, and soon after pulled my job as a tennis instructor."

"Didn't you go to the authorities?"

"My father did. I didn't want to run the risk of being exposed. But after the London police got their warrant and searched Jillian's, all the evidence was gone. It angered my dad so much, he's been investigating Jillian's since. Until he died. Oh, sure, they detained Terrence and held him for questioning. He came up with some phony alibi. But I've got him now. He still works there, and he's still doing his scam.''

''If Terrence was only questioned, what brought on the first trial?''

''Old man Jillian started to realize he was missing a few thousand pounds here and there. Somebody anonymously tipped him off with a phony receipt. But Jillian wasn't able to produce conclusive testimony against Terrence. The case was stonewalled on insufficient evidence.''

''So why did you try to get my father to support the book?''

''I've got nothing personal against your father, Amanda. If he would stop being so stubborn for once I'd have explained the whole thing. I wanted to include his testimony of innocence before we went to final print. But he wouldn't have it. He wanted nothing to do with the book—or me—because of the possibility of you finding out. That was the argument he and I had the morning before you came to the cabin. It's now apparent that he thought I was the one writing my father's books. No wonder he's held so much against me.''

Amanda pieced the facts in her mind, remembering Brandon's calls to the shop, her father's heated mandate to have him arrested, the cause for Brandon's second name, and the urgent call from Mick Terrence to her father. They all fit perfectly, for the first time.

"Your father will have to tell his story this time, though."

"But he's not been called. He's only there to support Terrence."

"Is that what you think? Your father couldn't care less about Terrence. He's there to make sure his own name doesn't fill the news—to keep you from finding out. The reporters will keep an innocent slant as long as he shows."

"If he doesn't care about Terrence, why would he bother to testify?"

"I'm having him subpoenaed."

"You *what?*" She paled.

"I had to. When I bought the business I learned he and Mick worked together most of the nights the laundering occurred. Jonathan's signature was on some of the receipts. I'm sure Terrence forged them, Amanda, but . . . your father *knows* something. It's time he told his story."

"But he lives in America. You can't subpoena him!"

Brandon nodded his head. "I can if he's visiting England."

She felt faint. "You said you thought he was innocent."

"I do. I have no doubt he'll be let go. But I need the information that he's not telling anyone. The court will be able to get it out of him."

"They'll squeeze the life out of him! How can you do such a thing?"

"Because it's the only way I can corner Terrence. I'm certain Jonathan knows about more than the money. I think he also knows of Terrence's plans to have me murdered. I need Jonathan's testimony to prove it.''

"If he does know, they'll suspect him of being an accomplice.''

The telephone rang, disrupting their quarrel. Brandon reentered the living room to answer it. Amanda listened to his one-way conversation.

"Yes . . . I see . . . Good. No, that won't be a problem. Thank you.''

Brandon hung up the receiver. He came over to stand beside her, sympathetically looking in her eyes.

"The London police have your father.''

Tears sprang behind her eyes. She willed them to stay back.

"He's scheduled for trial Monday morning. I'm going to fly over tonight; after all, they're my charges.'' He paused. "Come with me, Amanda.''

She walked back onto the deck and slunk down in the patio chair—the same chair where Brandon had massaged all of her anxieties away last night. Now they'd returned tenfold. But there was only one option. She had to go. She needed to be there to support her father. And Brandon.

Brandon squatted beside her, sitting on his heels. "Amanda? You have to believe your father is innocent. I believe with all my heart that he is.''

"And if he's not?'' The possibility made her burn with shame and one tear which she'd successfully locked in now fell, splattering on her palm.

"Let's hope he is.'' Brandon tenderly enfolded her hands under his own.

"All right. I'll go.'' She gave up fighting him and just

decided to accept things. Brandon was right. He was always right. If her father had nothing to hide there was no reason to worry. Yet, was he hiding something?

''Why don't you call Sara and explain things to her, so she doesn't get wind of rumors first,'' he advised her.

Amanda rehashed the sordid details to Sara, asking her to pack a suitcase before they arrived. She explained Brandon was making the hotel and flight arrangements. Then, making one more brief, vague call to Benjamin, she gave him the safe combination, telling him she would be away and that he was responsible for everything until she returned. She knew he was very capable of running the entire business. *Thank goodness Olivia is back at the stables,* she thought, *or we'd be in a worse mess!*

As their plane taxied the runway waiting for takeoff, Amanda thought the boarding time at Kennedy Airport took extremely long. Or maybe it just seemed so with her worries. Fortunately, she already had a passport from her recent move, and Brandon still had his from his trip to purchase Jillian's.

''There's something I don't quite understand.'' She shifted in her seat.

''What's that?''

''You purchased the publishing house after Daddy left, right?''

''Right.''

''But Mick Terrence doesn't know that you're the new owner?''

''No. With my name legally changed, none of the paperwork is under Derrek Madison.''

"But he'd likely recognize you, if he saw you again?"

"Sure."

"So if you were in England, purchasing Jillian's and going over the bookkeeping, how did you keep Terrence from knowing it was you? He replaced Daddy as manager, and would alone have access to the financial records."

"True, *but* he's no longer manager. I immediately handed Terrence a backseat on the job. He certainly deserved a cut in salary."

She laughed. "You didn't."

"I did. I demoted him immediately, with good reason. He's not worth a penny he's paid. He's been taking unauthorized paid leave for business that hasn't been recorded on any documentation. Besides, it was the only way I could get him out of management and pave the way for me to investigate."

"You're positively cunning!"

"Yeah, but I almost blew it. He was working overtime one night when I stopped by. Luckily, I made it out the door unnoticed and came back around midnight. I'm glad I did too. That night I found most of my evidence."

"How much do you have?"

"Enough to convict him of years' worth of stealing."

"Then why do you need my father to testify?"

"Because I need a witness who's been working at Jillian's besides Terrence. And, like I said, I'm sure your father knows about the arrangement Terrence made to have me killed. *That* I don't have evidence for."

Brandon was interrupted by the static-filled announcement of their departure from Kennedy Airport. The plane moved onto the taxi strip. Amanda inhaled a steadying breath. She hadn't expected to return to London so soon.

In the dim cabin Amanda absorbed herself in watching the peaceful lights of London. They twinkled in the blackness as the plane circled the grand city. A wave of nostalgia rushed through her. Brandon had been asleep for hours and she glanced at him, wanting to show him the lights. But seeing his handsome face nestled in the pillow, his five-o'clock shadow accentuated by the faint lighting, she decided against waking him. He looked too comfortable.

She continued her watch, soothed by the tranquil scene. As they neared the city, Brandon eventually stirred and let out a yawn. ''Did you think you'd ever go back?'' He stretched his arms and rubbed his eyes.

''I never gave it much thought, actually. Do you miss it? You lived there a while, didn't you?''

''Only a few years. Jeannie and I moved here when our mother died from diabetes. My parents had divorced and Dad followed his dream to London to buy his own publishing house.'' Brandon yawned and repositioned himself.

''When the police gave up on our former complaints against Terrence, Dad flew out to Charlottesville to pay me a visit. He liked Virginia so much he purchased some land. He said he was going to retire there, but the stress from his job interfered. After two bypasses he died from a heart attack.''

Amanda ached to comfort Brandon. ''I'm so sorry,'' she said.

''Thanks. Me too, for your mother.'' He paused, observing her face. "You really are the image of her, Amanda. Your mother was very beautiful, and a delightful person. You're just like her."

"Did you know her too?"

"Briefly. I met her on one occasion."

"When?"

"In England, a long time ago . . ." he said, pausing with a tiny smile.

"And? What? Tell me." She nudged his arm, anxious to hear the rest.

"At the club, outside of Rochester. Remember when your father was attending a seminar and you were all alone, keeping busy by trying to teach yourself how to play tennis? Remember when your mother picked you up at the courts to take you riding because your father had to attend the dinner party? Seeing her was exactly like looking at you right now."

The deeper meaning of Brandon's explanation finally hit her. "*You* were the instructor—the nice young man who gave me all those tips?" Amanda squealed, and heads turned to show disapproval.

"Derrek Madison at the time, but it was me, just the same."

"Of course," she whispered. She raised a hand to her temple. "All this time—I thought I was going crazy. I kept thinking how familiar you looked, but I didn't—I couldn't place where. And yet I thought I had met you, but I wasn't sure. I started to believe that déjà vu was real."

Brandon chuckled at her.

"And *you* never bothered to tell me about it, after all this time. Even when I told you this story at my tennis lesson. You and your multitude of secrets!'' Her elation swiftly veered into a rebuke for being left out again.

He smiled. ''I couldn't. That would have given everything away.''

''I am so *tired* of having to figure things out with you, Brandon.'' She was losing the restraint on her voice.

''Amanda, shh. Keep your—''

''If you leave me in the dark one more time, I swear I'll—''

Brandon kissed her, muting her protest. Warm and soft, his lips annihilated her tirade, supplanting it with longing. She responded to him easily this time. It was anguish to restrain her feelings any longer. If she tried, he'd surely remind her of her confession the night before. He wrapped his arms around her in the darkened cabin, tightening his embrace. She relished the sweetness of his kiss, melting completely.

Glaring lights ruined their privacy, and the pilot's voice aired a jumbled declaration of their arrival in fifteen minutes. Amanda rested her head in the warm nook of Brandon's shoulder, shielding her unadjusted eyes, still enjoying the tingle in her lips. *I must be in love. I melt whenever he touches me,* she thought dreamily.

Their taxi pulled into the hotel at twenty past three. The black London sky showed a hazy moon and the air held a slight chill.

Brandon paid the driver and they finally walked inside the hotel. He approached the desk for check-in and informed the clerk of his name.

The man gave him paperwork to sign, then handed a key to Brandon. A bellboy appeared as though on cue to take their bags, although Amanda had no idea where he materialized from. Together they walked one flight and stopped three doors down. Brandon tipped the bell-boy. The young man turned to leave.

"Wait!" Amanda tugged the young man's arm. "Where's the other room?"

Brandon looked at her with tired eyes, his hair still mussed from sleeping on the plane. She noticed the bell-boy was turning red.

"There isn't one, Amanda. We were fortunate to get this from a cancellation. Downtown London is booked in the summer."

"But—" She glanced at the bellman, who now graciously faced away from them, then she lowered her voice. "I am *not* sleeping with you in one room."

"Yes, you are. You have no other choice." Brandon kissed her on the nose, and motioned the bellman to continue on his way.

Amanda reluctantly followed him inside, unnerved by these recurring predicaments. It annoyed her that he always came out ahead in these discussions. Moreover, she doubted whether their situation was really a bind—or had he planned it to look that way?

Brandon shut the suite's large double doors and locked them.

Silence hung between them. She looked around hopefully. Maybe there was a cot or chesterfield he could sleep on. Fatigued from their journey, she plopped onto the love seat, which would have made a suitable bed if it were long enough to lie on. Not a chance he'd consent to sleeping on it.

"There's always the floor." She sighed.

"Pardon?" He laughed.

"You may sleep on the floor, since you never bothered to ask me before making such arrangements."

"I am not sleeping on the floor, Amanda, he countered, undoing his shirt and unpacking his suitcase. "You'll be perfectly safe with me. I'm too exhausted to even try anything with you."

She regarded him skeptically. "Well, then *I'm* sleeping on the floor." Then she picked up her suitcase and retreated to the bathroom with a brisk clamp of the door latch. She brushed her teeth and groomed all the tangles out of her long, black hair. When she emerged from the bathroom, Brandon had also changed and was wearing the gray silk robe that he'd worn while making her breakfast the morning before. He gave her a tired smile and exchanged places with her. Amanda hurried to turn off the light. Not knowing about the single room, she had packed only her favorite silk nightgown. She slinked under a blanket taken from the bed, nuzzling a feather pillow. A yawn escaped. Brandon returned and she could hear the swishing sounds of him removing his robe.

Amanda stiffened. He'd better sleep in something decent. She curled the covers tighter around her. Brandon crawled into bed. She lay rigid as a log, finding it impossible to relax.

"Amanda?" His groggy voice was close. He reached down and stroked her hair.

Her anxiety mounted. "Hmm?" she barely breathed a response.

" 'Night . . . sweet."

His breathing slowed to a steady rate. Amanda waited,

sensing he wanted to say something—but didn't. After a few minutes she couldn't ward off sleep any longer.

" 'Morning, princess."

Amanda smelled something wonderfully fresh and limy. She slatted open one eyelid to see Brandon sitting on the edge of the bed, cleanshaven and ready for the trial. He looked at her, warm and enticingly.

"Oh, no. What time . . . is it?" she spoke mid-yawn.

"Eight-thirty. We slept in a little. I have to meet with Ethan Trummel, Jillian's barrister, before they begin today's session."

"Why is it they've not needed you before now?" She sat up.

"Jillian filed the suit based on the evidence I found after my acquisition. Because he bothered to do the legal part, I agreed to let him receive the damages, since the pilfering has been coming out of his pocket for the last decade. We agreed I wouldn't cross-claim for damages as the new owner. I didn't want to attend the trial at all, but now it's inevitable."

"This gets more confusing each day."

"That's because you haven't been involved, until now."

"How long do you think it will last?"

"Today's session? About four-thirty."

"No, the trial."

"I'm not certain. There was talk of moving to the crown court. That's why I need to meet with the barrister, to get briefed on things."

Brandon stood from the bed to check his tie in the dresser mirror, then he grabbed his briefcase. "I'll be back to pick you up in an hour. I've ordered breakfast. It should be here in a few minutes. See you." He smiled sweetly, then left her in silence.

Amanda wished she could talk to her father, but she knew it wasn't possible. She would see him soon—on the stand—whether he was ready to see her or not. Dragging herself into the bathroom, she took a hot shower to wake up. As she emerged, she saw her breakfast in the living room. She viewed the elegant arrangement of muffins and strawberries, graced by two long-stemmed red roses, the daily paper, and a note. She slid the note from its tiny envelope: *Please trust me, Amanda. I only want the best for you.*

She tucked the note in her purse and turned to stare at her two clothing choices in the closet. Brandon's message hung like a fog in her mind. How did he always know what she was feeling? She donned her navy-blue suit with a dusty-rose blouse. Then, after her best attempt at French-braiding her hair, she sat down to eat. Amanda gazed at the food. She was tired, not hungry. Sipping her tea, she fingered through the paper just a page when she spied a headline on the trial. *Book House Scandal Moves to Crown Court—Jury to Decide.* It detailed the major events and gave the reporter's conclusion of how the whole event was likely to end up in a guilty verdict.

She set the paper down. Foreboding slithered in. She questioned whether Brandon was doing the right thing by her father. How sympathetic would a jury be toward someone who allegedly left the country knowing about the pilfering, and possibly, murder? She clenched her hands, praying her father was not an accomplice. Now disturbed by the article, she ate only a couple of strawberries, leaving the rest of her food untouched.

At ten o'clock sharp, Brandon called for her from the lobby. She met him eagerly and showed him the news article as their taxi wound through traffic toward the courthouse. She fidgeted with her purse straps as he read.

"Yeah. Ethan Trummel and I were discussing this."

"What does he think?"

"He wouldn't allude to a whole lot. Just that today's session could be a major turning point, *after* your father testifies."

She blanched. "So, they *are* going to call him today?"

"Seems so. Trummel also mentioned that the information I brought is going to be helpful in deciding the verdict."

"What information?"

"My father's book. The only problem is . . . it may not make your father look too good in the process."

"So, what's the difference between the book telling all and my father having to bare his soul?"

"Your father could have exposed the situation easily a long time ago, and made his side of the story public. I've never said the jury will be understanding of his silence. They may choose to believe the defense's story that he was paid off, or actually part of the laundering. Especially since he put in nine more years of service and the money kept disappearing."

"I wish you'd thought of this before."

"I did. I just didn't think it was all that likely, until this morning's meeting. By the way, I've already arranged for Jillian's barrister to tell your father about your attendance. We didn't want Jonathan to stumble on his testimony when he sees you in the courtroom. He knows, now, that you are here and fully aware of what's happening.''

''Does he know I came with you?''

''No. I assumed you'd prefer it that way.''

She sighed nervously, tugging on her purse straps again.

''Amanda, the best thing you can do right now is be supportive, no matter what happens. I still think everything is going to work out. We just have to trust Trummel to nullify the defense's accomplice-image tactic.''

She wanted to believe him. But his reassurance did nothing to calm her. She remained silent until they arrived, only peering out the taxi window.

''You okay?'' He looked her over. ''You look kind of pale.''

''I'll be fine.''

They shuffled into the stuffy courtroom and seated themselves. Amanda saw the defense counselor call Mick Terrence. Throughout the barrister's questioning, Terrence told his alibis for poor records and mismanaged money, claiming he had little ability to pull off such a scandal, and purporting that Jonathan—manager at the time—was a more likely suspect. The courtroom murmured in response.

''How dare he blame Daddy!'' Amanda whispered in Brandon's ear.

''I figured he'd try something low. I hope he didn't sway the jury.''

The barrister continued in Mick's defense, nearly painting him the picture of a saint. Amanda bit her lip to keep quiet, tense from her rising anger. At the end of defense's questioning Trummel took his turn to cross-examine. His interrogation seemed competent to Amanda, but somehow Terrence always weaseled away from the truth.

The judge finally called for a lunch break and the courtroom bustled out in commotion. "Hungry?" Brandon asked her, buttoning up his suit jacket.

"I'll go with you," Amanda said, "but I won't be very good company."

Brandon looked at her sympathetically. His eyes held a genuine compassion, but her worries badgered her. It was easier to pass the time in silence than discuss the matter. Besides, food only made her more nauseated.

They found a local restaurant and Brandon ordered. The service was quick, fortunately, helping to pass the time. Amanda watched passersby through the window.

Brandon finished his sandwich and sipped his coffee. "When this is over, there's something important I'd like to discuss with you."

"You mean *if* it ends, don't you?"

"That's inevitable. Don't let it destroy you. Keep a positive outlook."

"How can you say that? My father may be facing prison!"

"That's just what I mean, Amanda. You've got to have some faith in your father. You still think he's innocent, don't you?"

"They're doing him an injustice back there. After all of those lies, even *I* have doubts about him. How's the jury going to believe him now?"

Brandon gazed at her solemnly, then reached for a

napkin to wipe his mouth and hands. He gave no answer to console her. "We'd better get back."

The judge returned from his chambers and the defense barrister stood. "We call Jonathan Chambers to the witness stand."

Amanda thought she'd prepared herself mentally, but her skyrocketing emotions released a queasiness in her stomach. Brandon clasped her hand and squeezed it. She didn't mind his protective efforts now. She needed them. Fears pressed in. Her father looked horrified. She pitied him. Then he met her gaze. She shivered. Her world grew fuzzy, spinning. Black.

Amanda stared through blurriness. Finally she saw Brandon's blue eyes, showing concern. On a bench in the courtroom hallway, she managed to sit, supported by Brandon's arms. "I'm not sure I can go back in there. She put a hand to her head, feeling the spinning sensation again.

"You're not. I've called a taxi and I'm taking you back to the hotel."

At the hotel Brandon walked her to the room, then to bed. Laying her down in her clothes he covered her, then kissed her softly on the lips. "Get some rest. I'll be back around five."

Keys jangled in the lock. Amanda awoke as Brandon entered the room.

"Hi." He sat beside her, brushing the hair from her face, smiling warmly. "How're you doing?"

"Better. Hungry. How did it go?" she ventured warily.

"They put Terrence in a corner with my evidence. His barrister alluded to your father forging the receipts, instead of Mick. So they called a handwriting analyst to review the signatures. It's over, Amanda. Your father's innocent. Terrence is going to prison."

Now Amanda was awake. "That's remarkable!" She squealed and hugged him. "But . . . that means you had to testify. You jeopardized your life."

He nodded. "I couldn't stand to see them lie about your father. Besides, after he testified about overhearing Terrence's call to hire a killer for me, it had to be substantiated by something. I knew I had to take a stand. Now Terrence will face a second trial for Jeannie's murder."

"So, Daddy *did* know about it?"

Brandon nodded his head, watching her intently, and his expression turned somber. "He asked about you."

Her apprehension returned. Her heartbeat tripped. "What'd you say?"

Brandon frowned. "The truth. He didn't seem mad, just said he wanted to see you. He's waiting downstairs in the lobby."

"You told him I stayed with you?"

Brandon nodded. "I explained it was aboveboard."

She scooted off the bed and brushed her hair. She freshened her makeup and left for the downstairs lobby. Nearing the base of the stairs, she saw her father hunched in a velour chair, his hands together, fingers tapping in sync. She approached him and he noticed her.

"Hello, Daddy."

"Amand—" His voice broke, and he embraced her with tears in his eyes. "I'm sorry, dear. I never wanted you to be involved with any of this.''

''It's all right.'' She couldn't keep her own tears from cascading down. ''I'm so glad it's over. Now you can forget about it.''

''Yes.'' He pulled a handkerchief from his pocket and blew his nose. ''Well, you ready to go? I've arranged an extra seat on the flight home.''

Her thoughts immediately returned to Brandon. She sensed her father still had reservations about her maturity. An argument now would be embarrassing, and futile. Besides, she'd only come here with Brandon because it was necessary. Though her heart tugged her to stay with him, there was no reason to. Was there?

''Let me get my things. Maybe you could send up a bellman for me?''

Returning to her room, she caught the knowing look on Brandon's face, but she still needed to tell him her decision. ''I'm going back with him.''

''I figured you would.''

''Don't be offended.'' She began packing her suitcase.

''No problem,'' he responded in a low voice, taking another swallow.

The bellman knocked and soon trudged out with her suitcase. Amanda turned to Brandon. ''I'm not sure of what to say. Things are still spinning.''

''Don't bother,'' he cut her off, and looked out the window. ''Go on. He's waiting for you.''

''No—really. I'm grateful for what you did. You risked everything by exposing your identity for my father's sake. That was commendable. But—''

''Listen to me, Amanda.'' He turned abruptly and

pulled her into his arms. His gaze showed earnest desire, a wild need borderline to desperation. Her hair fell away from her face. He leaned so close, close enough to kiss her. "I didn't do all of this for me or your father . . . I did it for you. Don't you see how much I care for you, and want to be with you, Amanda?"

With that he lowered his lips to press firmly against hers. She ached for his kiss, had longed for it since they were on the plane for London. For one brief moment she allowed herself the pleasure of his love, and put her fears aside. But the memory of her father seeped in. Anguish returned.

She pulled back, looking up into his eyes. Her throat constricted with the pain of separation . . . but she had no choice. "Good-bye, Brandon."

Emotions pressed in. They clawed at her heart, challenged her reasoning. She battled them and hurried out the door. Down the hall, she retrieved a tissue to quell the tears. She tried to forget the desperate look in his eyes. She reminded herself this was best. No matter what Brandon had sacrificed for her father, Jonathan Chambers would never approve of Brandon. And she needed her father's support to start her own stables.

Chapter Twelve

Amanda stood by the dining-room window. She stared out at the early September morning. Sunshine caused the trees to glow with vibrant gold and orange and red. She looked back at her stable plans spread across the dining-room table, shaking her head in disbelief. *I wish I could tell Brandon.* She wanted to share her victory with him. More so, she longed to see him again. Every day, since the Fourth of July, the aching grew. She hadn't expected the emptiness would be so consuming when she'd said good-bye in the Grosvenor Hotel. But it had. Outwardly she appeared normal but inwardly her heart was breaking. As she perused the groundwork plans for her dream come true, she was amazed at how everything had turned out.

Almost everything. The aching continued.

"I can't believe he agreed," she muttered, still bewildered. She sat down with Sara and sipped her Earl Grey tea. Having just shown the plans to her father and explained all her ideas, she'd expected the worse—only to hear his enthusiastic approval instead.

But loneliness spread like a disease that consumed her soul. Often, Amanda wondered if she'd paid too costly a price in exchange for her dreams.

Sara smiled proudly. Her round face beamed with encouragement. "He just saw how sensible your plans are. How could he not agree with them?"

"Amazing. He's barely spoken to me since I quit ballet a month ago. Finally, I get the nerve to bare my heart's desire and—without asking a single question—he agrees to the whole idea." She shook her head. "And that grin on his face. I don't understand, Sara." Amanda drummed her fingers on the rosewood table. "Something's changed. He even wants to attend the auction with me."

"Your mother said his scars would heal. They did." Sara's reminder was punctuated by the telephone. She bustled to answer it in the hallway.

Sara poked her head through the doorway. "For you. Mr. Cordell."

Amanda shivered. Her chair scraped sharply on the wood floor as she hurried to take the call.

She stood over the phone. Now was the time, she was convinced. She loved Brandon. She'd known from the day she saw his paradise. But she'd had to follow her dream. Brandon had told her he'd wanted that too, though it had meant hurting him.

Yet now that her father was offering support for her venture, she realized the stakes had been too high. Catching her dreams hadn't been worth the cost of sacrificing love. All she wanted now was to repair the damage. She wanted Brandon. And she would trade her dream to have him.

"Hello?" Nerves made her hands tremble.

"Amanda," Brandon's familiar voice resounded.

She closed her eyes, relishing the deep sound of it. She'd yearned to hear him say her name again. "Yes?" She tried to keep the butterflies in her stomach at bay.

"I know it's not like me to call. I hope I'm not disrupting you."

"Not at all." Since the trial, she'd wished a thousand times that he would call. "How are you?"

"Fine. I just wondered if you'd drive down to the cabin. There's something I wanted to show you, and . . . I wanted to . . . say good-bye."

Good-bye? Warnings flashed in her heart. She clamped her arm around her stomach. Her breathing grew choppy. Nausea crept in.

"If it's too much to ask, I understand, but I really hoped to see you again. If that's okay?"

"Yes, Brandon. I'll leave right away."

She drove the distance nonstop, anxious to see him and distressed over his good-bye. Had he found someone else? Or was he merely cutting the cords between them because she had pulled away? She fought the apprehension that knotted her midsection, praying for one more chance to admit to him what she'd finally admitted to herself—she loved him.

The BMW's tires crunched along the gravel drive, winding through the dogwood-lined road to Brandon's paradise. She cut the engine and retrieved her keys, shaking her head at the thought of hiring the locksmith again.

Inside the cabin, she checked each room for Brandon but only found them stocked with furniture and half-empty boxes. He was nowhere. She crossed the living room and checked the back deck. Outside, she heard the thwack of tennis balls. She remembered the hidden courts and followed the trail to them.

He noticed her arrival, smiled, and raised his T-shirt hem to wipe his forehead. ''You made it.''

The gesture briefly exposed his tanned chest. Amanda swallowed and tried to speak. ''Y-yes.'' She also smiled, very happy to see him again.

''Let me wash up. It'll only take a minute. I'll meet you on the porch.'' With that, he kissed her cheek and sprinted up the trail.

Amanda brushed her cheek, wishing he hadn't done that. The absence of his lips was not as punishing as feeling them again—warm and tender—and knowing it would be the last time. She wandered up the path and sat on the deck chair. The hills lay abreast on the horizon, subtly exchanging their summer greens for fiery orange and bright yellow leaves.

He approached her from behind, holding two tall glasses of lemonade. She admired his quick change into white shorts and a fresh dark-purple shirt. His hair, now combed, tamed all but the sable curls at his neck.

She caught a scent of aftershave. Why'd he bother? Didn't he realize that saying good-bye would do her in? He handed her a glass and leaned against the pine-log deck railing. His dashing smile had disappeared with his tennis attire, and he watched her with distinct concentration.

Amanda stiffened. *No. Don't say it. I can't bear to lose you now.* Waves of uneasiness swelled inside her. She nervously sipped her drink. She desperately wanted to end the silence, but was afraid of hearing what was next. Brandon made matters worse by looking so compassionate, apologetic.

"Let's take a little walk," he said, and started down the porch steps.

Amanda followed, and they kept silent. That was fine with her. She didn't want to hear that dreadful word. *Good-bye.* It was so unfair. Just when she was ready to trade everything to have him, he was going to sever the cords between them.

They stopped at the love-seat swing, now surrounded by thick, new grass. Brandon sat and her eyes lingered on the space beside him. "Amanda, please—sit down. You're making me nervous."

She caught the sincerity in his eyes. Relenting her jittery stance, she sat stiffly and braced for her confession. It was worth a try, she concluded.

"Brandon, I know why you asked me to come here, but there's something I want to say first, if I may."

He faced her squarely, propping his arm on the back of the swing and brushing her hair from her face. At his caress, Amanda's thoughts shifted gears. How she'd missed his touch. She tried to focus on her tennis shoes, to concentrate, so the words would come out the way she intended.

"What you did for my father, or rather for me . . . I want you to know that I'm—both of us are grateful. You endangered your life, and I'm very thankful that you cared enough to do that. I know it must have hurt to recount your sister's death.'' He waited silently. She wondered if he sensed that there was more.

Squarely facing him, her heart pounded fiercely. *Say it—now! Or you'll never get another chance.*

''I've done a tremendous amount of thinking, about things, and . . . about us. You have different plans now, but I—''

''Amanda, what is it?''

''I've ached, being away from you. Every waking moment I've seen you, or heard you, or felt you. When you called today, I had to see you, to tell you. . . . I love you, Brandon. I can't bear to lose you again.'' She stared down at her laced fingers. And waited.

He tenderly lifted her chin. With his forefinger he traced lightly from the dip behind her earlobe down to her lips.

She felt lost in his gaze. He appeared relieved—and concerned. The dam broke that restrained her emotions, and tears flowed down her cheeks.

Brandon smiled. He took her by the hand, leading her up the path toward the house, saying nothing. But then he led her down the other side of the house, on another new trail.

''Where are we going?'' She wiped the tears from her face. But he remained silent, towing her along. They came to a clearing. Amanda froze.

Their sudden approach startled the horse that contentedly ate from the combine. It whinnied. Then the sleek black animal swung its head in excitement and trotted in circles, expecting a ride.

Amanda gaped. Her muscles were paralyzed with shock. What should she say? He obviously wanted her to know. She patted Brittany on the neck, rubbing her muzzle. Then, she looked at Brandon in utter dismay.

"Amanda? Do you remember when we first had that drink in the clubhouse, and I told you about my paradise, that I had built it for someone like you?"

She numbly nodded, too overcome to fully comprehend his meaning.

"Well, you may not have believed me at the time, but I meant what I said. I built this cabin with you in mind. True, I never expected to see you after meeting you in England. It didn't matter then, because you were too young in comparison.

"But last year, when I caught word your father was planning to buy a publishing house here and move the two of you to America, it drove me crazy. I was rebuilding this cabin at the time. I'd never forgotten what a sweet girl you were, and I was consumed with seeing you again. Once the cabin was finished I realized I'd practically constructed it hoping you'd be able to share it with me. You can't imagine how stunned I was when you signed up for lessons at the club." He laughed.

She stared in awe, still enveloped in surprise.

"I also knew that your father's past would stand in the way." Brandon's expression was sincere. "I never wanted to hurt you, or give you any cause to think the worst of me. When we were in London, I realized you'd been through too much. I doubted you would ever be able to trust me, or understand how I loved you. At that moment, I honestly thought it was over."

He drew near to her, taking her hand, holding it

tightly. She gazed into his blue eyes, felt the warmth and strength of his grasp. "I left England convinced you would never admit what I knew you felt in your heart. But I'd already made arrangements to purchase Brittany. She was to be your wedding present. I guess, I really would have been calling to say good-bye if you'd declined coming here. But when you said yes, I knew there was a chance." He slipped a sparkling diamond ring onto her finger, and she watched the motion in astonishment. "I've been waiting a long time, Amanda. Will you marry me?"

She beheld his earnest gaze. Then she stared again at the glimmering ring, feeling the contortion of so many feelings gripping her heart.

"The two of us are yours for life." Brandon scratched Brittany's velvety black muzzle. "*If* you'll say yes."

The barrier in Amanda's throat finally broke. "Yes, Brandon! Yes!" She squealed deliriously and wrapped her arms around his neck. Her legs dangled as he hugged her tight.

She could feel him burying his face in her hair. Finally, he lowered her to the ground and kissed her. The eagerness in his lips fueled her simmering desires. She had waited long for his love and ached for all of it. His hands stroked her sides, sending tides of yearning through her.

Yet, slowly, he curbed his roving caresses, pulling away from her. "I can wait," he breathed into her ear. "Not for long, but until we walk the aisle. It'll be wonderful," he whispered, and kissed her nose.

She finally relaxed in his embrace, sighing, feeling the heat from his chest, knowing that he really loved her.

Brandon held her around the waist and started to chuckle. "I'm glad you said yes. Your father and I had our doubts. He's ecstatic about turning the press over to Benjamin and working at the stables as a partner, but if you—"

"What? He's never mentioned that."

"He warned me, all right. He knew that you were all on your own with the decision to marry me."

"Are you saying my father *already knows* about this?" Her annoyance flared with the sudden information.

Brandon nodded. "Yeah. I guess I've finally gained his admiration. I don't want to start off on a bad foot with my father-in-law."

"You two had this proposal all figured out? Behind my back?"

"You really had me worried, though. Like I said, we had our doubts."

Her annoyance transformed into playful fighting. Placing her leg behind his, she tripped him backwards onto the ground and sat upon him.

"No more secrets, Brandon! I can't take it anymore." She tickled him, watching him twist around in the soft grass. "I won't put up with it—except for birthdays, and Christmas, and anniversaries. Promise?"

Brandon finally caught his breath. "Okay, okay! I promise. No more secrets. Now . . . it's your turn." He wrestled her onto her back, pinning her easily beneath his weight. She labored in vain to free herself.

"You've certainly become the independent woman you wanted to be." He managed to curtail her struggling.

"Now, promise me you'll always love me. Because I love you so very much, Amanda."

Amanda ceased her tussling and smiled, losing her steam in the passion of Brandon's eyes. "I promise."